KID STUFF

KID STUFF

great toys from our childhood

David Hoffman

photography by Viktor Budnick

CHRONICLE BOOKS

SAN FRANCISCO

Library of Congress Cataloging-in-Publication Data:

Hoffman, David, 1953–

Kid stuff : great toys from our childhood / David Hoffman :

principal photography by Viktor Budnik.

p.   cm.

ISBN 0-8118-1162-X

1. Toys   I. Title.

NK9509.H64 1996

688.7'2—dc20   95-25457

CIP

Printed in Hong Kong.

Distributed in Canda by Raincoast Books

8680 Cambie Street

Vancouver, B.C. V6P 6M9

10 9 8 7 6 5 4 3 2

Chronicle Books

85 Second Street

San Francisco, CA 94105

Web Site: www.chronbooks.com

for

may you stay forever young

CONTENTS:

When you get right down to it

it all started with Noland Harper.

He was the kid who lived around the corner, and in 1960 my parents forced me to go to his birthday party. Noland (or Skipper, as his family used to call him) was a year younger, and being in the first grade the last thing I wanted to do was spend the afternoon with a bunch of kindergartners. But lured by the promise of ice cream and cake, I dragged myself away from the TV and I went. Good thing. Because it was there I saw my first Slinky.

Someone—I think it was Debbie Dickens—had brought it as a gift. Probably because Noland was more preoccupied with his Roy Rogers double holster set (or maybe because he was extremely mild-mannered), his new toy got taken out of the box and passed around. I wasn't sure what to expect after Bill Hill finished and handed it to me. But within seconds, I was mesmerized, whelmed by how magical it felt as it rhythmically flowed from one palm to the other.

When I got home, it was all I could talk about. And as I closed my eyes to go to sleep that night, the only thing I saw was that steel coil, my head filled with memories of its smooth moves and soothing sounds.

Before you finish the story yourself—jump to the conclusion that I squirreled away my allowance, gave up bubble gum and comic books, and a few weeks later rode my bike to Shadwell's Drug Store where I bought a Slinky of my own—let me set the record straight. I never had to do that. Because by the next afternoon, my parents had already gone out and gotten a Slinky for me. I remember I was standing in the dining room when they surprised me with it. I remember it had nothing to do with it being *my* birthday. I remember shaking, I was so excited. But most of all, I remember that they did it without my ever even asking.

As kids, toys were our center and our solace. It isn't hard to understand why; no matter how little we were, with toys, we were in control. We may have been too young to cross the street alone, but alone in our bedrooms or dens, we could be the parent, make a million, or rule entire worlds.

Which also explains why, years later—as we second-guess lives and double-think careers—each of us has our own 'Rosebud'; that single toy that is a one-way ticket back to simpler times. Of course it doesn't have to be a sled (though if it is, chances are good it's one stamped with a red eagle and labeled Flexible Flyer). It could just as easily be a wad of pink goo that lifts images off the pages of the Sunday funnies, a box of plastic face parts that you stick into a potato, or a dual-control drawing board where writing your name or making a circle is a major artistic achievement.

A word or two about the classics covered in these pages: Each had to be older than twenty-five years and at the same time, currently marketed and available. Okay, so maybe *They're not what they used to be*. (Purists take note: changes—in design, materials, or packaging—are usually the result of higher production costs and stricter safety regulations). But at least they're still here.

Second, the choices, while personal, are not without purpose. I wanted to avoid fads, the kind of toys that come and go in cycles, but have no year-in, year-out staying power (so no Hula Hoops or Troll Dolls). I also opted not to include those products that have tapped into the kids' market with a scaled down "junior version" of the original (which ruled out some well-loved board games like Scrabble and Clue).

I decided to omit anything that pushed the nostalgia button, but had actually been off the store shelves longer than it had ever been on (Betsy Wetsy, for example, which was only recently reintroduced). And I rejected generic items (such as teddy bears, pick-up-sticks, or roller skates) except where one company had released the staple by which all others have been judged.

They started as mere amusements and later became big business. From Ant Farms to Wiffle Balls, Legos to Lionel, mainstream, mass-market toys have evolved into icons of popular culture. Still, who knew that Lincoln Logs were invented by the son of Frank Lloyd Wright, that Barbie had a last name (it's Roberts), or that the Play-Doh brand modelling compound was actually formulated as a non-toxic substance to clean wallpaper?

Here, then, is a guide to all the favorites of our past, dedicated to anyone (whether a Boomer or a Slacker, whether it was the Beaver or the Bradys) for whom "Go to your room and play" meant Cootie, Colorforms, and a giant box of 64 Crayolas with a sharpener in the back.

ant farm

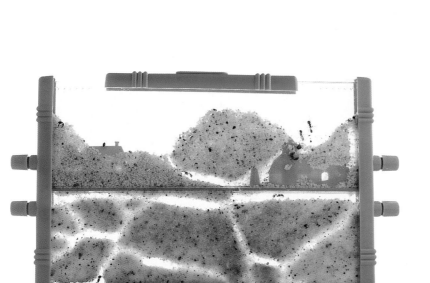

ANT FARM

It was 1956 and Milton Levine, owner of a mail-order novelty company (the same one that saturated our comic books with deals for "a hundred cowboys & Indians—or a hundred WWII soldiers—or a hundred circus animals—all for only a buck!"), was sitting poolside at a July 4th barbecue at his sister's home in Southern California. The sight of a colony of ants inching towards the food table brought back memories of the fun he had had as a child in Pittsburgh—scooping ants into Mason jars filled with sand and watching them dig—and got him to thinking: Why not put together a formicarium for kids?

To test his idea, he mocked up a sample (by modifying a clear plastic Kleenex dispenser), then took out a display ad in the Home section of the Sunday *Los Angeles Times*. When the response made it clear that he was on to something, Levine went to work finalizing the actual design. His biggest problem was giving the item the sense of a toy; so inspired by a drawing he had seen in his niece's coloring book, he added a miniature panorama of a rural countryside and (in a stroke of pure genius) dubbed himself Uncle Milton and his new product an Ant Farm.

Success came quickly, spreading from toy stores to pet shops (where it was heralded as the perfect low-maintenance companion: no vet bills, no baths, no late night walks) to schools, libraries, and museums. Fifteen million farms (and three-quarters of a billion ants) later, what you get now is the same as it was then: two sheets of clear plastic held upright by a green plastic frame with a barn, windmill, and farmhouse as detailed and familiar as a Norman Rockwell painting, along with a stock certificate that, once mailed back, guarantees a supply of thirty to thirty-five ants. Only the sand has changed, and that has increased the ants' longevity from just three months to more than eight.

About those ants. Send in that certificate and what Uncle Milton sends you is a container filled with *pogonomyrmex californicus*—red ants (harvester ants) from the California desert. Though once caught with a special high-tech ant vacuum, they are now caught the old-fashioned way: by blowing into ant holes with a straw, then by scooping them up with jars as they come running out.

These ants are preferable over any you could catch yourself because they are one of the few types among the world's 9,000 species that actually work—that is, they dig—during daylight; they're big enough in size (a quarter of an inch) that they aren't able to escape through the air holes at the top of the Ant Farm frame (see, Mom, I told you so); and they won't breed. That's because male ants don't do well in captivity so only the females are sent (but never the queen because there just aren't enough of those to go around—and even if there were, California agricultural regulations prohibit it).

Although trademarked, the name Ant Farm was adopted with Levine's blessing in 1968 by a group of designers from San Francisco who were pioneers in "underground architecture." That's underground as in "avant garde" and in the literal sense, since these were the guys who, inspired by their namesake, buried ten vintage Caddys (nose down, tail fins straight up, and at the same angle as the Cheops's pyramids) in a wheat field off of Interstate 40, west of Amarillo, Texas, and came up with Cadillac Ranch. Talk about your bumper crop.

Barbie

The tale is almost as well known as the end result: How in 1950 Ruth Handler would take her nine-year-old daughter Barbara to the five-and-dime shopping for paper dolls, then watch as she would bring them home, cut out the clothes and dress them up. Considering Handler's history (she and husband Elliott—along with a partner, Harold Mattson—had founded Mattel Toys) it was only a matter of time before the obvious struck: Why not manufacture a three-dimensional version of a paper doll? No one argued that the concept was revolutionary, but her all-male staff of designers resisted, saying American mothers would never buy a doll with breasts.

So the idea languished until 1957, when Handler, on vacation in Vienna, saw a display of sharply dressed adult dolls in a store window. The Lilly Doll, as it was known, was (unbeknownst to Handler) based on a racy character from a German comic strip, and she bought two: one for Barbara, and one for the designers back in Hawthorne, California. Using it as a model, Mattel spent three years creating their own unique version. In the end, it stood $11 1/2$ inches, had vinyl skin, rooted hair, and was—because Ruth Handler persisted—moderately anatomically correct.

To name the doll, she took her daughter's nickname. And in March 1959, dressed in a zebra-striped bathing suit, Barbie met her public.

The Barbie Time Line:

1959 Introduced in a test market in nine states, Barbie's first face has a fashion-model aloofness, with arched eyebrows, a sideways glance, and a seductive pout. Perceived as a little too sophisticated, she is repainted (thereby softening her look) when Mattel begins mass production the next year.

1962 Following Jackie Kennedy's popularity as First Lady, Barbie gets a bubble haircut and a haute couture wardrobe.

1967 Forced to compete with the Beatles, Barbie goes mod: longer face, long straight hair, real eyelashes and—thanks to a more malleable plastic—a twist-and-turn waist.

1971 Meet Malibu Barbie. Her face is not only tanned, but has also been restructured. She now smiles.

1977 Barbie as we know her today. The smile has been widened (to include lots of teeth), there are sun-streaks in her hair, and she comes packaged wearing dresses instead of swimsuits.

Make-up and hair color changes are one thing, but it is the multiple professional careers and ethnic rebirths that account for the ninety different Barbies that are created annually. The most popular version to date: Totally Hair Barbie (with tresses from head to toe), which was introduced in 1992.

Barbie has spawned collectors clubs, an annual national convention (the highlight is a style show where participants wear life-size Barbie outfits), and a high-gloss magazine (*Barbie Bazaar*, with 40,000 subscribers). But so have other toys. What Barbie has, however, that others don't is her own museum: The Barbie Hall of Fame. Owner Evelyn Burkhalter has assembled a collection that is one accessory away from being 100 percent complete (What's missing? The stuffed toy poodle that came with the 1972 black print Poodle Doodle outfit). Which means she's got over 20,000 pieces divided into sections (such as Barbie brides), arranged chronologically (all the better for tracking how fashion, hair, and lifestyles have changed since 1959), and packed floor to ceiling in a 3,000-square-foot space. *433 Waverly Street, Palo Alto, California. (415) 326-5841.*

Barbie Slept Here (well, sort of). At The Venice Beach House, a nine-room inn in a restored seaside Southern California craftsman home, Cora's Corner—a suite that's all peach and antique white wicker (with a great old iron bed)—so impressed an executive from Mattel that it served as the model for Barbie's Town House. *15 30th Avenue, Venice, California. (310) 823-1966.*

Two Barbie dolls are sold every second somewhere in the world.

Ninety-five percent of all girls in the United States (between the ages of three and ten) have at least one Barbie; the average girl has eight.

The very first Barbie is identifiable by the copper-lined holes in her feet, where she fit onto her stand.

And attention trivia fans. Barbie's last name is Roberts, her middle name is Millicent, her parents are George and Margaret, and she went to Willow High School (which is where she met Ken Carson).

Forget blonde vs. brunette. The bigger Barbie question is: bimbo or feminist? Figure on one hand you've got the classic airhead, totally preoccupied with clothes and looks, who teaches girls that all it takes to be what you want to be—regardless of whether it's a ballerina, astronaut, rock star, surgeon, or president—is the right outfit. But on the other, Barbie doesn't define herself in relation to children or family.

She lives in a world where she is the center, where she comes first and where men (in her case, Ken) are nothing but another accessory.

COLORFORMS

Essentially it's your basic starving artists' story. In 1951, two students, married couple Harry and Patricia Kislevitz, were experimenting with various materials and mediums, particularly—given their financial status—anything that might be available to them at little or no cost. Which not only explains why the bathroom in their New York City apartment was painted in a hideous shade of orange (the price was right) but why a friend in the pocketbook business passed on a large roll of flexible vinyl (he didn't want it, but thought they might be able to incorporate it into some project or idea).

Was he ever right. Noticing that scraps of the vinyl would automatically stick to the semi-gloss paint in the bathroom, Harry and Patricia cut out basic shapes and combined them to decorate the wall. Then they left sheets of the vinyl—along with a pair of scissors—out on a counter, as an invitation to their guests to do the same. Everyone had so much fun adding to, rearranging, and redoing this giant collage, that the Kislevitzes decided to market their idea. They started by creating a series of flat vinyl cut-outs (standard geometric shapes in primary colors), then packaged them, along with a sheet of laminated paperboard, in an oversized black box because, Patricia pointed out, expensive jewels always came in black boxes. They called their brainchild Colorforms.

It caught on big, but soon squares, triangles, and circles weren't enough. Shapes gave way to characters. In these new sets, pieces were die-cut and screened to look like familiar faces or everyday objects; workboards doubled as background dioramas. You could bake cakes and set the table in Miss Cooky's Kitchen, dress Popeye's little buddy according to the weather, recreate entire scenes from favorite TV shows and movies. And you could do it all without scissors, paste, or paint.

The Colorforms' emblem—part character trademark, part design logo—was the work of Paul Rand, who was also responsible for creating the look for IBM, UPS, and (the revised) GE. Introduced in the early 1960s, this particular design is one of the most recognizable product symbols in the toy industry today.

No other toy appealed to all five senses like Crayolas did. Was there ever anything more beautiful that the sight of a newly opened box—each

crayola crayons

stick standing straight up, perfectly in place, like an army of color ready for action? Remember how good it felt just to grab a fistful and write your name (or scribble madly) with a whole bunch all at once? Or the way, if you colored until layers built up, the crayon would *pop* when you took it off the paper? Granted, crayons tasted like a cross between soap flakes and those wax lips sold at Halloween (kids with more discerning palates preferred Play-Doh). But that smell is so memorable that according to a Yale University study it is among the twenty scents most recognizable to American adults (the first two being coffee and peanut butter), and so soothing that sniffing Crayolas has been proven to lower blood pressure.

When Edwin Binney took over his father's Peekskill Chemical plant in 1885 and teamed up with his cousin C. Harold Smith, they not only changed the name, but used twenty years of experience with pigments and other coloring compounds to create a line of retail products. Chief among them: shoe polish, printing ink, and slate pencils.

It was these pencils that introduced Binney & Smith to the educational market. When teachers complained about the chalk they had been supplied with, the company's chemists came up with a dustless version. From there, they drew their way straight into the children's art field. Hearing that the best crayons to be found were European and too expensive for most schools to buy, they took a wax marker they had recently invented (to label the various crates and barrels around the factory) and adapted the basic black formula to a non-toxic variety of colors. Binney's wife, Alice, having been a teacher, saw the importance in this project and it was she who combined the the French word *craie*—for "chalk"—with "olea" from *oleaginous*, meaning "oily," to name what would become their signature product.

Crayola colors may change (the line now includes 112 different shades) but their names rarely do. The two exceptions: Prussian blue (which in 1958 became midnight blue in response to teacher recommendations that kids could no longer relate to Prussian history) and the very popular flesh (more accurately re-labeled peach in 1962, in recognition that not everyone's flesh was the same shade).

All Crayola crayon names appear on labels in lower case because tests reveal that lowercase letters are easiest for elementary school students to read.

Binney & Smith offers a free, 60-minute factory tour—very much designed with kids in mind—which includes a look at the complete manufacturing and packaging processes, a visit to the Crayola Hall of Fame (a sort of mini-museum), and a complimentary coloring book, stickers, and box of crayons when you're done.

For more information, call (610) 515-8000. Or write Crayola Product Tours, 1100 Church Lane, P.O. Box 431, Easton, Pennsylvania 18044.

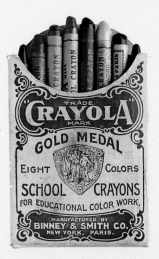

The first box of eight (above)—packed in the now-classic yellow-and-green carton—was introduced in 1903 and included the same red, blue, yellow, green, violet, orange, black, and brown you'll find in the 8-box today (below).

DUNCAN

yo-yo

Centuries ago, natives in the Philippine Islands would fashion primitive hunting tools, tying a long plant vine or strip of animal hide to a softball-sized piece of rock. Designed so that when hurled, it could be easily retrieved from a safe distance, the weapon evolved: first into a more complicated version that would retract with the flick of a wrist, then, scaled down, into a kids' toy. Both were called by same name: Yo-Yo, which means "come back" in Tagalog, the native language of the Philippines.

In 1927, Pedro Flores, a Filipino busboy at a hotel in Santa Monica, would amuse guests by performing tricks with his handcrafted yo-yos. Besieged by requests, he had begun making and marketing them when businessman Donald Duncan spotted him and offered to buy him out. Though he popularized it, Duncan's yo-yo was not the first dual-discs-on-a-string-plaything. Yo-yo type toys are the second-oldest known toy (after dolls) in the world, dating back to China (forget wood—these were ivory with satin cords) and ancient Greece (those were terra-cotta).

Later, they spread to France (where they helped amuse Napoleon's soldiers between battles) and England. Encrusted with jewels or painted with geometric patterns, they were a popular diversion with the European royal courts.

From the '30s into the '60s, Duncan had the world on a string. Demonstrators would go from town to town, wearing white cardigan sweaters, working two yo-yos at once, making all of us believe we could be champions. The tricks we watched in awe had catchy names, and at school and after school, we practiced hours on end (with a Tournament, Imperial, or the easier-to-hold-and-control Butterfly) until we could rock the baby, walk the dog, or go around the world.

Duncan trademarked the word *yo-yo* back in 1932, so competitors were forced to call their products Royal Return Tops, Whirl a Gigs, or Cheerios. However, their efforts to challenge his claim to the trademark mounted over the years, and in 1965 the company, financially drained by legal expenses (and over-extended by advertising costs), was forced into bankruptcy. What was left of the business was purchased by Flambeau Products, who had been making plastic yo-yos for Duncan and had the molds and equipment to continue. Though basically reduced to an advertising or promotional premium in the '70s and '80s, in the '90s yo-yos have come bouncing back. Partially due to the fact that once again they are a staple on school playgrounds—this time, because Duncan has created a five-part hands-on science program where students use yo-yos to form hypotheses, test theories, and collect data.

When the Duncan Yo-Yo Man first appeared on the package in 1929, most of the models were carved from hardwoods such as maple, ash, or beech. Later, some were metal; the first plastic version wasn't introduced until 1957.

To promote business for his new company, Duncan went—uninvited and unannounced—to see publisher William Randolph Hearst. He talked his way past the front door and proposed an arrangement: Hearst's newspapers would advertise Duncan-sponsored yo-yo contests in which kids would compete for bicycles and sports equipment. In return, Duncan would require competitors to obtain three new subscriptions as their entry fee. It wasn't just Hearst who responded favorably. A thirty-day campaign in the *Philadelphia Daily News* alone sold more than three million yo-yos.

Donald Duncan was also responsible for inventing the parking meter and introducing the Good Humor "ice cream on a stick."

Easy-Bake Oven

By the time the '60s rolled around, boys' rooms were filled with a wide range of great "boy toys"—from Lionel Trains and Erector Sets to Matchbox Cars and G.I. Joe. For girls, however, it was another story. Of the items marketed specifically to them, many were mundane (like jacks or jump ropes) and those that weren't, were dolls. But all that took a turn in 1963, when Kenner hit on a way that girls could not only have their cake—they could bake (and eat) it, too.

The idea came from the company's New York sales manager, who, inspired by the pretzel vendors on every corner in Manhattan, brought to the management group his suggestion for a mini-pretzel maker. Play kitchens had long been a playroom staple, but up until now they had been just that: play. His notion was that the toy really worked. Not only did everyone agree, but the pretzel maker evolved into an actual mini-oven (styled to look just like Mom's), and the possible products it could bake grew to include cakes, cookies, candy, brownies, biscuits, pies, and pizzas.

The real recipe for success was not just that it worked, but how. Knowing that parents wouldn't buy anything they deemed too dangerous, Kenner's designers chose to avoid a traditional cooking element and developed an oven that baked solely using the heat generated from two ordinary 100-watt lightbulbs. It wasn't that the toy didn't get hot; it was the notion that the primary component was an object kids were exposed to everyday that gave it the feeling of being safe. So much so that the company originally wanted to call it the Safety-Bake Oven. But when the National Association of Broadcasters informed Kenner that they could not advertise it on television as such since the name implied a degree of safety it hadn't been proven to have, they chose to go with Easy-Bake Oven. Over three decades later, it remains (not counting dolls) the number one activity toy among girls, and having outlasted a host of imitators (remember Susie Homemaker?), it is as all-American as the apple pie it can create.

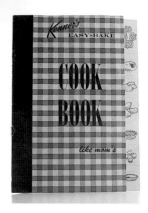

Although its concept has remained the same throughout the years, the styling of the Easy-Bake Oven has changed to keep pace with the times. The original—in all of its turquoise, June Cleaver splendor—led to double ovens and black "magi-glas" viewing windows in the '70s and a more streamlined, digital, microwave look in the '90s.

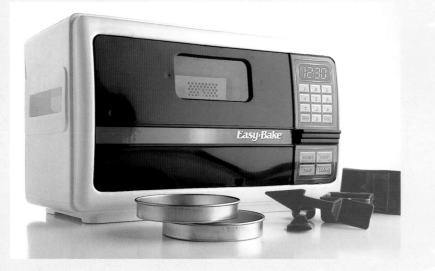

When first introduced, Easy-Bake came with its own cookbook and its own line of baking mixes. After purchasing Kenner in the late '60s, General Mills realized they had the perfect vehicle for establishing long-term brand-name identification, and for over fifteen years the oven was packaged with miniature boxed versions of their famous Betty Crocker products.

Though the first to do it with success, Kenner wasn't the initial toy company to recognize the potential of a working miniature stove for girls. Ironically, Lionel also did—thirty-four years earlier when the entire back cover of the 1930 catalog was devoted to a "real electric range." The design was impressive (it featured two burners, a porcelain finish, and a built-in thermometer), but at $29.50 it cost more than a real electric sewing machine or vacuum cleaner, and almost as much as a full-size gas stove. Far too expensive for the Depression market, the toy fizzled and quickly disappeared.

erector set

Fresh out of Yale Medical School, A. C. Gilbert turned down an internship and, along with a friend (John Petrie), formed Mysto, a company that manufactured magic tricks. In 1911, as head of marketing, Gilbert would make frequent train trips from their New Haven offices into New York City to meet with department and toy store buyers. Week after week, he'd watch as workers along the railroad line erected an electrical system out of steel girders that had been riveted together. Aware that there was a lack of affordable quality toys on the general market and wanting to expand his company's line, one day it all came together: kids love things they can build (witness their fascination with blocks). So why not a toy construction set with girders, panels, wheels, pulleys, gears, and a small electric motor?

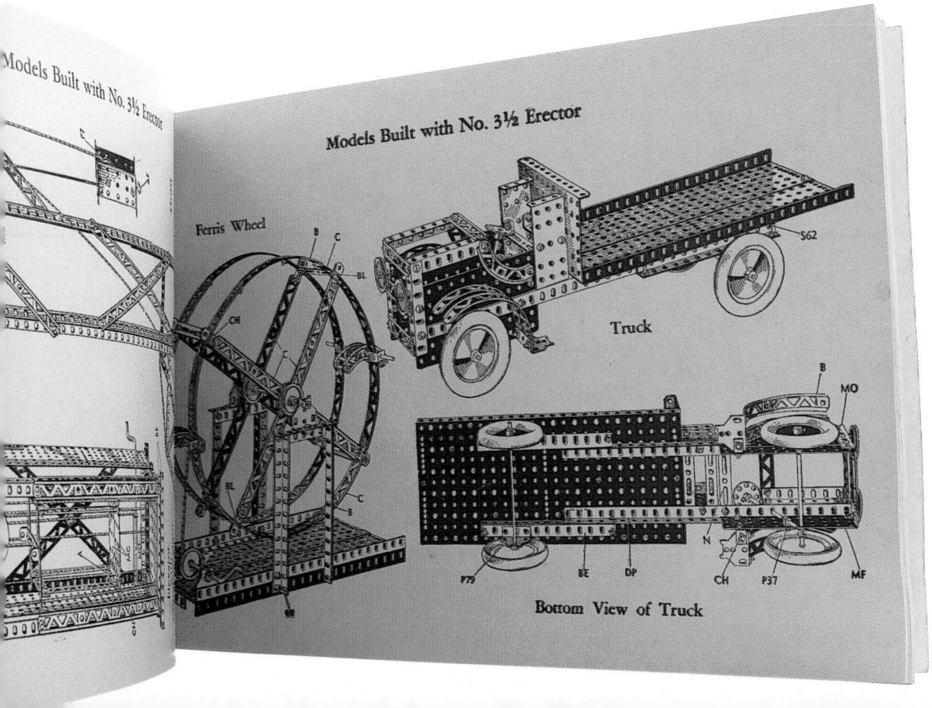
Models Built with No. 3½ Erector
Models Built with No. 3½ Erector
Ferris Wheel
Truck
Bottom View of Truck

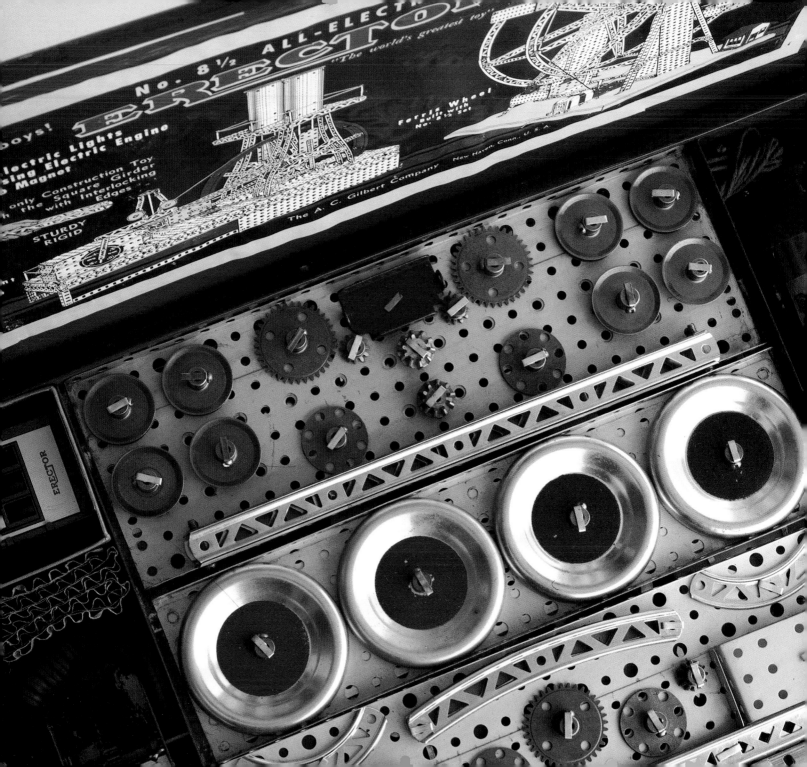

Gilbert went home, where he cut sample pieces out of cardboard, then took those to the shop the next day and had a craftsman replicate the prototypes in tin. Using nuts and bolts, he randomly fashioned them together, and the Erector Set was born. After perfecting the product over a period of one year, he launched it in 1913, with the first major advertising campaign ever done for a toy. National magazines—from the *Saturday Evening Post* to *Good Housekeeping* and *Popular Mechanics*—targeted fathers and sons with the catchphrase, "Hello Boys! Make Lots of Toys." And that they did.

Gilbert manufactured Erector for fifty years, offering a range of sets each season, in several different sizes. He revised the design of the pieces in 1924, and also started the practice of including parts that would only build a particular model—a truck, steam shovel, Zeppelin, or locomotive.

During this period, most of the boxes were (as they had been since the beginning) wood, often elaborate 9-drawer oak cabinets weighing as much as 150 pounds. Metal boxes painted different colors were introduced in 1933; by the 1950s, just about all the boxes were the classic red most of us remember.

In addition to being a doctor, an accomplished magician, and the inventor of the Erector Set (all by the age of twenty-six), A. C. Gilbert was a gold medalist in pole-vaulting at the 1908 London Olympics. Not to mention that in 1917, he actually saved Christmas.

The story goes that the U.S. Council for National Defense, in order to conserve wood and metal for wartime use, proposed an embargo on the buying and selling of any holiday gifts. They urged toy manufacturers to cut back on their most popular products and asked parents to support their efforts by putting their money into war bonds instead of presents for their kids.

Knowing that no Christmas sales would destroy them, a group of manufacturers headed to Washington, armed with Erector Sets and Tinkertoys. Gilbert eloquently pleaded their case, then distributed the samples. From the moment they got their hands on them the cabinet members were kids again, assembling endless metal and wooden structures. "Toys appeal to the heart of every one of us, no matter how old we are," announced one of the Secretaries. And with that, the council reversed their decision.

In the early '60s, milk carton–style cardboard boxes and plastic parts were introduced. Sales dropped and eventually Erector Sets disappeared from the marketplace. After a ten-year lapse, the license was acquired in 1990 by Meccano, makers of a top-selling building toy in Europe. The quality is excellent, but baby boomers beware: the pieces are totally different in look and shape from what you found in the sets of the 1950s.

The same view that inspired Gilbert in 1911 can still be seen today, traveling on the Metro North, aboard the New Haven–Harlem line.

Paul Chasse was a garage mechanic in the Kremlin-Bicetre area of Paris whose talent for tinkering was geared towards cars—until 1958,

etch a sketch

when he rigged up an automatic drawing toy that didn't need batteries and had no loose parts. Although his *"L'Ecran Magique"* (or Magic Screen) stirred up great interest when first demonstrated in Germany, it was promptly rejected by the numerous manufacturers who saw it—including Howie Winzeler of Ohio Art—due mainly to the fact that Chasse wanted too much money for the rights.

The item might not have gone anywhere if it hadn't have been for a junior executive at Winzeler's company, who six months later did his brother-in-law a favor and set up a meeting for him to show a prototype he represented to the VP of Sales. None of them had any idea that the idea they were meeting about had already been passed on by the boss. Which was good, because only when the VP brought it to his attention for a second time did Winzeler decide that even at $25,000 (five times more than he had ever paid to license anything) Magic Screen was worth the chance.

Chasse's toy, previously only made by hand, underwent redevelopment, reworking, and ultimately a name change—to Etch A Sketch—before mass manufacturing began on July 12, 1960. Even then, for the first few months, production line problems meant that at least one out of every four units had to be scrapped. They were tossed in a garbage dump outside of Bryan (the city where Ohio Art is head-quartered) until company executives realized that locals were picking up the rejects and taking them back to toy and department stores for cash refunds.

Times have changed, but unlike most classic toys, Etch A Sketch really hasn't. The only difference since 1960 is in the knobs, which were originally brass, then plastic, and are now mounted flush to the red frame, with a beveled edge, for easier handling and control. Of course, there was the limited edition Executive Etch A Sketch, introduced in 1985. Made of sterling silver, with sapphires and topazes encrusted in the turning knobs, it came packaged in a velvet-lined mahogany box and sold for $3,750.

The Way It Works:

The screen's reverse side is coated with a gray-colored mixture of aluminum powder and plastic beads. A metal stylus connects to both turning knobs; that enables it to be moved either up and down or left and right. As the stylus moves, it dislodges the powder mixture from the window, causing lines to appear where the mixture had been (kind of like what happens when you use your finger to write your name in the dust on the car windshield). Shake the box, and the mixture is redistributed evenly again, causing the lines to disappear.

While most of us beamed at just being able to draw a circle, numerous artists—including the late Elaine de Kooning—have used the Etch A Sketch as their canvas. Boulder, Colorado, graphic designer Jeff Gagliardi is known for his reproductions of great masterpieces, from Mona Lisa to American Gothic, while Nicole Falzone's specialty is portraits—including celebrities like Jay Leno, David Letterman, and Jim Carey. Their works of art (which average around $250) are made permanent by drilling small holes in the back of the Etch A Sketch to remove the powder, then by spraying a fixative on the underside of the glass.

Jeff Gagliardi: (303) 494-7605. Nicole Falzone: (310) 306-7020.

flexible **FLYER**

CHILDHOOD MEMORIES OF WINTER PROBABLY WOULD BE LIMITED TO SHOVELING
sidewalks—or sweating in wool overcoats that itched unforgivably—if it hadn't been for Samuel Leeds
Allen, a Quaker whose namesake Philadelphia company was a leading manufacturer of farm equipment
that he invented. Problem was, while business was booming, it was
largely seasonal. So in an effort to keep his factory workers employed
(and to prevent them from leaving to take other jobs and not coming
back), Allen searched for an additional product, one that could be
manufactured in fall and sold for winter. Drawing on his lifelong passion
for "coasting" on the icy sloping lawn of the family's New Jersey
farm—with his father, his classmates, and ultimately his own kids—the
logical answer was a sled. In 1889, after a number of experiments
and prototypes, he replaced wooden runners with flexible steel ones,
attached a moveable, steerable crossbar, added a slatted seat, and
christened his version the "Flexible Flyer."

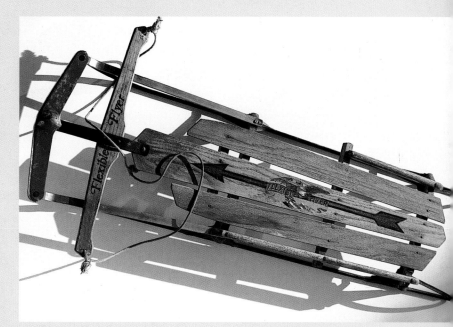

With its signature red eagle trademark, the Flexible Flyer may be
immediately recognizable today, but it actually took another five
years to catch on. Department store buyers were wary, saying that it
wasn't practical. And Allen's own employees didn't want to push it
because the sales season interfered with their vacations. But eventually, thanks primarily to the increased
popularity of skating and tobogganing, there was a revised interest in winter outdoor sports. Timing *was*
everything, and sales of Allen's sled soon surpassed those of all the other competitors combined.

**As a businessman, Allen was a dream boss. He introduced the concept of death and disability insurance, and
implemented the first employee retirement plan.**

frisbee

During the 1920s, students at Yale invented a game of catch in which instead of balls, they tossed around metal pie tins from the Frisbie Baking Company in nearby Bridgeport, Connecticut, yelling out "Frisbie!" to alert passersby to an approaching airborne tin. More than twenty years later, Fred Morrison, whose father had invented the automobile sealed beam headlight, came up with a gimmick of his own: a circular, nearly flat, plastic disc that when thrown in the air seemed to hover and float. Morrison sold his saucer-shaped creation to the Wham-O toy company, who in early 1957, relying on the public's fascination with UFOs and men from outer space, released it as the "Pluto Platter." The toy did moderately well, but appeared to be more of a passing fad (in the shadow of the craze created by Wham-O's other big product, the Hula Hoop) until, hearing about the game being played on the Yale campus, executives dropped the space-age name and adopted a new one: Frisbee.

The times were clearly on their side. In the coming years, America had had its fill of war and violence, and peaceful competition struck a chord. By the end of the decade, there was not only an International Frisbee Association, this simple piece of plastic spawned an organized team sport, an accredited university P.E. class, a Cub Scout activity badge, and a tool (to keep flares aloft) for the U.S. Navy.

Yalies delight in this story, but others aren't so quick to agree. Legend has it that Morrison, a Californian, might have gotten his inspiration from a Hollywood film set, where in the '30s, camera crews would lob film-can lids back and forth to keep themselves entertained on long shoots. Still, some speculate that the Frisbee's true origins were at the very spot where it later gained its biggest following: the beaches. Forget surfing. For kids in Southern California in the '40s, a popular pastime was taking the tops from empty coffee and paint cans and seeing how far they could hurl them.

In early 1990, Wham-O donated a large quantity of Frisbees to an orphanage in Angola, Africa. Several months later, they received a letter from one of the nuns there, thanking them for "all the wonderful plates." She explained that not only had the kids been eating off the Frisbees, but they were also using them to fish, fetch water, and cart their things around. "And do you know what else?" she added. "Some of the children are even throwing them and playing catch."

The Game of Life

and other games

Talk about clouds having silver linings: In 1860, a man named Milton Bradley, a printer from Springfield, Massachusetts, saw sales of his popular lithograph of presidential nominee Abraham Lincoln plummet—all due to the fact that Honest Abe decided to grow a beard and Bradley's portrait featured him without it. Desperately seeking another product to keep his company afloat, Bradley went to press with The Checkered Game Of Life, a board game he had invented some years earlier. Its rules sent players on an altruistic path, where the first one to make it to "Happy Old Age" was the winner. Its resounding success put Milton Bradley in the game business.

A hundred years later, to celebrate (and promote) the company's anniversary, executives dusted off the old board (which had been out of production since the turn of the century), revised and revamped it, and created a 1960 edition they called The Game of Life. Like the original that inspired it, it was designed to reflect the times. Only this time, instead of choosing between right and wrong in hopes of finding happiness, players would go to college—then get a job—in hopes of becoming a millionaire.

In recent years, The Game of Life has been tweaked yet again. These days, players—on their way to getting filthy rich—are also rewarded for being politically correct: for recycling their trash, learning CPR, and saying "no" to drugs.

Cootie

Start to ask questions about a guy from Minnesota named Herb Schaper and you're likely to be told any number of things: how he was a barber (not true), a mail carrier (barely true—he did a short stint as a substitute), owned a children's store that sold toys that he had whittled out of wood (true), and loved to fish (absolutely true). So it stands to reason that while carving a lure in 1948, Schaper took a look at the ersatz bug creature he was creating and didn't see bait, but the makings of a great kids' game. Next, he had a mold cast from the original, and from that manufactured 600,000 plastic copies. Reminded of the slang term he had heard used for lice while serving in World War II, he adopted it as the toy's name: Cootie.

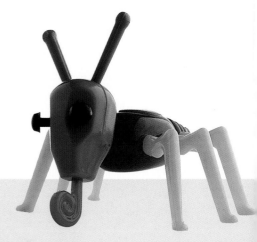

Not one to rest on his laurels, Schaper followed up with three other successful plastic games: Ants in the Pants, Don't Spill the Beans, and Don't Break the Ice. Then, using his newly found wealth, he started a new business. The product? Fishing rods.

Candy Land

Even as late as 1949, the games created and marketed specifically for kids were primarily skill tests or required little more than adding pieces to a puzzle. Traditional board games, although sold in toy stores, were usually designed with adults (or the entire family) in mind. But all that changed when Eleanor Abbott, a San Diego woman recuperating from polio, took her mind off her own ill health and busied herself with devising activities for kids who suffered from the same disease. One of her projects—a board game set in the Peppermint Stick Forest that required nothing more than the ability to match colors to play—was such a hit that she gave it a name, Candy Land, and submitted it to Milton Bradley. It was immediately accepted.

Yahtzee

A dice game dreamt up by a wealthy Canadian couple (as something to do aboard their boat) proved so popular with family and friends that they asked Edwin Lowe (the mastermind behind Bingo) if he would make up some samples for them to give as gifts. Lowe was so impressed with their "Yacht Game" that he offered to buy the rights. They agreed, sacrificing all future royalties for a few free copies of the game—a game Lowe manufactured and sold with great success under the catchier name, Yahtzee.

Twister

Back in 1965, Reyn Guyer was running a sales promotion firm he had founded with his father. Known for creating eye-catching in-store displays and innovative package design (clients included Pillsbury, Brach's Candies, 3M, and Kraft Foods), they were commissioned by a Wisconsin shoe polish company to develop a premium for use in a "send a buck and a box top" mail-in campaign. Guyer was toying with a notion that included color patches that went on kids' feet (along with a correspondingly colored walk-around grid), when it occurred to him that what he had come up with might work better as a game. He called on one of the company's artists, who sketched out a giant board, then tested it out with a group of office workers divided into two teams. Seeing the fun in eight people-as-playing pieces crammed on a 4x6 mat, a number of concepts emerged, eventually evolving into a game they called "Pretzel."

Pretzel was picked up by the Milton Bradley company, who, against Guyer's wishes, changed the name to Twister. But even with the name change, the game still had trouble once it got to market. Major retailers balked, not sure where it fit in or if customers would understand it. Company fears that they might have a huge flop on their hands vanished, however, on May 3, 1966, when Twister was featured on *The Tonight Show*. Helping matters was the fact that one of Carson's guests that night was Eva Gabor. All it took was one shot of Eva on her hands and knees, with Johnny climbing over her, and no longer was there any doubt what this game was all about. Further proof: during that first year alone, more than three million copies were sold.

G.I. JOE

IN 1962, LICENSING AGENT STANLEY WESTON APPROACHED HASBRO CREATIVE DIRECTOR

Don Levine with the idea of a product based on an upcoming TV series, *The Lieutenant.* Though hesitant

to tie a toy to a program that was geared to adults and might well be off the air in a year, company

executives were intrigued by what Weston proposed: a "doll" for boys (though never would they use

that word—this was an "action figure," thank you). Like Mattel's Barbie, this toy was designed to be

the center of a world of accessories. Hasbro promptly bought Weston out (reportedly for a flat fee of

$100,000), then, searching for a name, remembered a 1945 Robert Mitchum movie that had pop-

ularized the slang term used for American soldiers during World War II—*The Story of G.I. Joe.* Upon

spotting a poseable wooden mannequin in an art store window, Levine suggested that the figure bend

and move. The rest was easy: his hair would be black, brown, blonde, or red and painted on; his eyes

either blue or brown. And whereas Barbie had the latest fashions, Joe would have uniforms (for each

branch of the service), weapons (from hand grenades and flame throwers to M-1 rifles or bazookas),

and military gear (helmets, backpacks, and canteens).

If store buyers had their doubts (a doll by any other name was still a doll), the public didn't; by 1965,

G.I. Joe was the number one selling toy among kids five to twelve years old. And not just with boys. It

seems girls also wanted to play with him, particularly when he was dressed in his West Point or Annapolis

duds. In response, Hasbro introduced the G.I. Joe Nurse, who wore a Red Cross uniform and came with

medical supplies. She bombed, but (mint and in the box) can be worth as much as $5,000 today.

In 1969, with anti-war sentiment high and toy guns under attack, Joe's sales dropped dramatically.

Hasbro was quick to react. They cleverly transformed the former G.I. into an "adventurer," scaled him

down (first to 8, then to 3³/4 inches), and reinvented him as "Super Joe" and "A Real American Hero."

Over the next two decades he took on the identity of a hunter, an astronaut, a martial artist, and an eco-warrior with optional features such as life-like hair, bionic ligaments, and a Kung Fu grip. Still, the best Joe was the original Joe, and in 1992, he not only grew back to full size, but true to his beginnings, came dressed ready for active duty.

Before settling on the name *G.I. Joe*, Hasbro also considered a few others: Rocky the Marine Paratrooper, Skip the Navy Frogman, and Ace the Fighter Pilot.

When finally introduced, G.I. Joe was $11\,^1/_2$ inches tall, fully jointed with twenty-one moving parts, and dressed in fatigues. His face—with a scar on the right cheek to make him look more masculine—was (at least according to the initial press release) modeled after a composite drawing of twenty winners of the Congressional Medal of Honor.

A Talking G.I. Joe was released in 1967 (yank on his dog tag and he spouted eight battlefield commands) and if packaged in the gift set version, has long been the Joe most sought after by collectors. Talking Joe made headlines again in 1993, when the NY-based BLO (as in Barbie Liberation Organization) pirated a current shipment of both toys and switched his voice chip with her's. For this revised Joe, "Math is hard," while Barbie barked orders like, "Take the Jeep and get some ammo fast!"

Hasbro may not call G.I. Joe a doll, but the U.S. Customs Service does. Too bad. If classified as a toy soldier instead, it would not be subjected to a 12 percent tax when imported from the factory in Hong Kong.

hot wheels

Elliot Handler, one of the original founders of Mattel, decided in 1967 to capitalize on the popularity of miniature die-cast metal cars by adding die-cast and working wheels. What his development team came up with was a prototype that was gravity-powered and could reach a speed of 300 mph downhill. Upon eyeing their ultra-fast version in action, Handler exclaimed, "Wow, those are hot wheels." The name stuck.

Over 700 different models have been created since the first Hot Wheels, a Chevrolet Camaro, rolled off the Mattel assembly line that year. The best-selling vehicle, however, is the Chevrolet Corvette, while the most valued is a Volkswagen Beach Bomb. This van—if it's the one without side slots and with the surfboard sticking out the rear window—could, according to collectors, bring up to $4,000.

How They Do It:

Hot Wheels often undergo as much R&D as cars turned out by Detroit. The production process starts by photographing the original, making sure every detail is captured on film. Precise measurements are also taken, noting stats such as height, wheelbase, and engine compartment overhang. These photographs and specs are then sent to the engineering department where they are translated into mechanical drawings. Next the drawings are sent to a pattern maker who produces a wooden model, which is four times larger than the actual Hot Wheel vehicle will be. It's here that every detail is faithfully reproduced, from door handles and logos to the shape of a headlight or instrument panel. Finally, the model is taken to the shop, where the die-cast is injected into the mold and the body emerges. It is polished, washed, spray-painted and detailed, then the wheels, chassis, and engine are assembled. The final product is approximately three inches long and 1/64th scale to its real life counterpart.

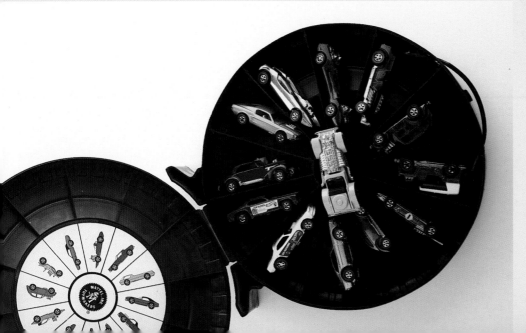

LABYRINTH

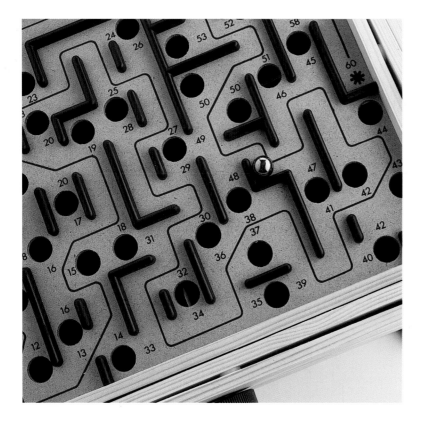

While hospitalized in Sweden for tuberculosis in the early 1940s, Tage Friberg kept busy—and kept his mind off his illness—thanks to a handheld skill game made for him by Sven Bergling, a family friend. Crafted of wood, it involved balancing a steel ball the size of a marble on a board. The rules, which Tage formulated over repeated plays, were simple: move the ball from one corner to the other by following a marked path, but circumventing a series of numbered holes. Fall in any one of the holes before reaching the end and that was it—the number represented your final score and the game was over.

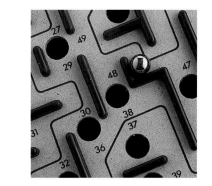

As Bergling had hoped, the hand-eye coordination and fine motor skills needed to play the game served as good rehabilitation therapy for Tage. What he didn't realize was that everyone else who watched Tage as he played would be so interested in trying the board for themselves that Tage would, once he had recovered and been released, propose a plan to produce and market it under the name *Labyrinth*.

To do this, he turned to another friend, Allan Carlsson, who worked at a plant that made wooden doors, and contracted him to fashion the various parts. After assembling the individual pieces together, Tage went house to house, peddling the game. Positive response eventually led to a deal with a Stockholm department store, where strong sales (6,000 pieces a year) and good word of mouth prompted the Brio Company to take over all distribution and introduce the product worldwide. Fifty years later, Labyrinth is not only still available from Brio but is still made exclusively for them in the Carlsson family factory. With only one minor change: the maze walls and control knobs, which were originally wood, are now constructed of plastic.

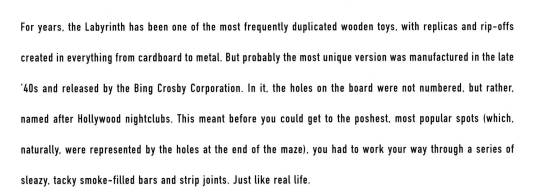

For years, the Labyrinth has been one of the most frequently duplicated wooden toys, with replicas and rip-offs created in everything from cardboard to metal. But probably the most unique version was manufactured in the late '40s and released by the Bing Crosby Corporation. In it, the holes on the board were not numbered, but rather, named after Hollywood nightclubs. This meant before you could get to the poshest, most popular spots (which, naturally, were represented by the holes at the end of the maze), you had to work your way through a series of sleazy, tacky smoke-filled bars and strip joints. Just like real life.

Lego

In 1932, Ole Kirk Christiansen, a carpenter from Billund, Denmark, compensated for his lack of work fixing houses by handcrafting wooden stepladders, ironing boards, and children's playthings to sell to the area's farmers. When he started making more money building animal pull-toys than he ever had building furniture (and realized as long as there were kids, there would be a need for toys), he decided to turn his attention to the toy business full time. He then pieced together the Danish words *leg godt*—which mean "play well"—to name his new company Lego.

Christiansen eventually expanded into plastic, including miniature tractors and baby rattles. In 1949, he introduced a product called Automatic Binding Bricks, a set of interlocking red and white blocks that had studs on top, were hollow underneath and could easily be stacked together. Five years (and three additional colors) later, buyers started asking for a complete toy system. At the urging of his son Godtfred, the bricks were renamed (to Lego Bricks), repackaged (in one of twenty-eight sets—some of which contained small cars, figures, and a cardboard "city map"), and redesigned (tubes were added underneath, to provide more play possibilities). Now, instead of simply being piled one directly on top of the other, two eight-stud bricks could be joined in twenty-four different ways. By the end of the 1950s, Lego bricks became one of the most popular toys in Europe; and in 1961, a limited number of sets were finally available in the United States.

Unbeknownst to Christiansen at the time he chose the name, lego also translates as "I put together" in Latin.

Today, the Lego company produces approximately 1,700 different shaped "bricks" (and over 400 sets) in a wide array of colors (including new shades, like green, gray, and black). The possibilities are endless, especially when you consider that six eight-stud bricks of the same color can be combined 102,981,500 ways.

Lego products are made of a plastic called Acrylonitrile Butadiene Styrene (ABS). During the manu- facturing process, the ABS is heated to the consistency of bread dough, then pressed together between molds, cooled, and ejected (all in about ten seconds). The procedure is so accurate that only twenty-six pieces for every one million produced have to be rejected.

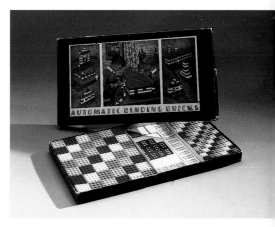

Legoland, a twenty-five acre theme park in Billund, Denmark, serves up the usual rides and attractions, but what sets this one apart are the models—an incredible array of buildings (the Parthenon and the U.S. Capital, for starters), animals (life-size antelopes, elephants, hippos, and zebras), monuments (Mt. Rushmore, the Statue of Liberty), and statuary (everyone from Hans Christian Andersen to Chief Sitting Bull), built, brick by brick, from the same sets found in toy stores. No special pieces, no computer-generated designs. The only variance is that pieces are glued together for safe keeping.

A U.S. Legoland will open in 1999 in Carlsbad, California, thirty miles north of San Diego. But a taste of what's to come can be discovered at the Lego Imagination Center at the Mall of America in Bloomington, Minnesota. The 7,000-square-foot attraction features sixty large-scale models (which change regularly), the only Lego store in the country (including, on occasion, sets usually not available outside Europe) and play area where kids can build their own creations. Mall of America, S-164 South Avenue, Bloomington, Minnesota. (612) 858-8949.

ON A 1916 TRIP TO TOKYO WITH HIS DAD (WHO HAPPENED TO BE FRANK LLOYD WRIGHT), John Lloyd Wright (also an architect) was particularly taken with a revolutionary technique (it involved interlocking beams) being implemented in his father's design for the Imperial Hotel. Though no doubt

LINCOLN LOGS

Lobby of Imperial Hotel

spurred by the recent success of Erector Sets and Tinkertoy construction systems, the younger Wright's fascination with watching workers lift timber into place was reportedly what inspired him to come up with his own building toy—a kit of miniature hardwood beams that could be joined together to assemble cabins, forts, and bridges. Capitalizing on Americans' romanticized feelings for earlier pioneer days and their esteem for Abraham Lincoln (who proved that anyone, no matter how humble their beginnings, could achieve greatness), Wright decided to call his creation Lincoln Logs. So convinced was he of the power of these two images to sell his product, he bucked traditional marketing practices and instead of featuring a photo of kids playing with the toy on the front of the box, the package bore a simple drawing of a log cabin, a small portrait of Lincoln, and the slogan "Interesting playthings typifying the spirit of America." Although Wright's plan worked and Lincoln Logs were a huge hit, their greatest success came in the 1950s, thanks to the frontier craze and anything evocative of Davy Crockett.

Shortly after inventing Lincoln Logs, Wright chose to refocus on his career as an architect. Still, other toy companies wasted no time capitalizing on the product's popularity, and soon store shelves were stocked with Lincoln Bricks and Lincoln Stones as well. In fact, the name became so popular that not all Baby Boomers who remember playing with Lincoln Logs actually ever did. What many of us had instead were Halsam's American Logs. These had a more realistic look but, always in the shadow of their predecessor, they were too often mistaken for it and eventually got lost in the marketplace.

Originally made of redwood, today's Lincoln Logs are produced from lighter color woods.

Lionel
trains

It was in early 1900 when twenty-two-year-old electronics whiz kid Joshua Cohen (who in later years would claim to be the inventor of the flashlight and the electric fan) sold Robert Ingersoll, a toy & novelty retailer in lower Manhattan, on the concept of a miniature electric railroad car. Initially the device (which actually looked more like an open cigar box than a boxcar once Cohen completed it) wasn't designed as a toy, but as window dressing—"an animated advertisement," he called it—to attract attention to Ingersoll's store. Cohen charged $4.00 for the gadget; the next day, Ingersoll needed another. Seems that the first person who saw the moving train car was indeed lured into his shop. The problem? Instead of buying the merchandise the train had been used to feature, he bought the train.

Ingersoll ordered six more and when other stores followed suit, Cohen incorporated, taking his middle name—Lionel—to name his new business venture.

Since that first Lionel appeared in Ingersoll's window, operating displays have remained a company tradition, getting more and more elaborate with time. From the mid-'20s to the early '60s, the New York showroom was lined with wall-to-wall layouts where bridges, tunnels, billboards, and rolling hills served as backdrop to realistic railroad scenes. Engines whistled and blew steam (thanks to a bottle of fifty smoke pellets), conveyors loaded coal via remote control, and in what would become the all-time favorite car, a tiny man popped out and delivered authentic silver milk cans, one by one, onto the platform. Wonderful as all that was, it pales to what you will find today in the company's Chesterfield, Michigan, Visitor's Center, where thirteen transformers power eight trains simultaneously on the ultimate 560-square-foot layout—complete with operating buttons that allow guests to control the action. The Center, which was built entirely by company volunteers, also features a large collection of memorabilia, a separate (and equally elaborate) setup just for kids, plus two additional trains that circle the perimeter of the building on tracks suspended from the ceiling.

For information, or to arrange a tour (admission is free, but reservations are required), call (810) 949-4100, extension 1211.

Each year, Lionel produces over one million engines, cabooses, and other railroad cars. Put together, they would make a toy train close to fifty miles long.

In the Lionel world, girls were almost nonexistent. When they did appear in print ads or catalog pages, they admired what their brothers were doing; rarely were they shown touching the trains and never was their hand on the controls. In 1957, fearing that they had overlooked a potential customer base, the company introduced what is now known as The Girl's Train, a pastel set "in fashion-right colors" (including a frosted pink locomotive) that flopped badly. What Lionel had failed to realize is that girls who wanted trains wanted the real thing. As a result, many of the pastel versions got spray painted black, making the original Girl's Train set—with it's buttercup yellow boxcar, sky blue caboose, and white-and-gold transformer—a collectible that's highly sought after today.

While the majority of model railroads in the early 1950s were found under (and around) Christmas trees (including the one in the Eisenhower White House), Lionel sets were constantly popping up elsewhere: like at the Cleveland medical lab (that relied on a GG-1 electric engine to transport radioactive radon the twenty-one feet between the storage room and laboratory, then used one of the ore-dumping cars to drop the radon capsule down a chute by remote control) and the California coffee shop (where hamburgers and ice cream sodas were served by a train that ran up and down the lunch counter, stopping in front of customers who removed their order before the train backed up and returned to the kitchen).

"Which— LIONEL do you want, Son?"

Magic
'**8**' BALL

The year was 1946. It seemed the hottest craze in the country was second-guessing the future. Drugstore scales didn't just tell you your weight; they spit out a card predicting what was going to happen to you next. People spent hours hunched over Ouija boards, restlessly waiting for them to spell out their sage advice. And no Chinese dinner was complete without the cookie created by the Hong Kong Noodle Company, the one that was baked, then stuffed with a strip of paper that had a fortune printed on it.

In Cincinnati, the Alabe Crafts Company worked to develop a novelty version of the crystal ball. While its conception is—appropriately enough—shrouded in mystery, what Abe Bookman came up with was a hard black plastic sphere the size of a grapefruit, which when turned upside down would reveal the answers to life's most perplexing issues.

The Way It Works:

Hand anyone a Magic '8' Ball and the question most frequently asked is not about the future, but what's inside the ball.

The Answer? The ball is actually two separate halves glued together (then polished to help make the seam disappear). Split it open and you'll find a plastic vial, affixed to one end and standing upright. About the size of a juice glass, the vial is filled with a blue liquid (more inside information: the liquid is a combination of water, blue coloring, and propylene glycol—an antifreeze to keep the solution from turning solid during shipping). Floating in the liquid is a polyhedron, whose twenty sides bear twenty different answers in raised letters. The clear plastic cap that seals the cylinder not only assures that the blue solution won't leak out, but doubles as the little window through which you view your answers.

Of the twenty possible answers, ten are positive, five negative, and five neutral. Which, according to statisticians, gives a high degree of accuracy to the ball's ability to forecast.

Currently there are three different Magic '8' Balls on the market: the original, a Spanish version, and—so you can, literally, listen to the voice of reason—one that talks.

Outside of a kid's playroom, the Magic '8' Ball is probably the most visible of classic toys. As proof, just turn on a television. Watch *Friends*, and you'll find one sitting permanently on Chandler Bing's office desk, just as, three decades earlier, one sat on Rob Petrie's office desk in *The Dick Van Dyke Show*. It has also been consulted by *Murphy Brown*, *Seinfeld*, and *The Simpsons*, has starred in a commercial for AT&T, and has been used by local newscasters to predict election outcomes.

magic rocks

The epitome of offers found at the back of comic books in the 1950s, Magic Rocks were the brainchild of a pair of entrepreneurial brothers in Southern California, James and Arthur Ingoldsby, who came up with the idea when they were doing an in-store demonstration in a downtown Los Angeles five-and-dime. There to hawk a vitamin pill for plants, they noticed that most of the crowd was gathered around a guy who was selling faintly colored crystals you grew inside a jar. Checking him out, they quickly realized that they could do what he was doing, only they could do it better. By 1945, the brothers had formulated their own version—which grew rocks in eight vibrant colors—and began marketing the "Magic Isle Undersea Garden."

Their hunch paid off. Their product did better and ultimately outlasted the one that had inspired them. Still hearing from buyers that the name was too long, too vague, and too hard to remember, in 1958 they simplified it to "Magic Rocks."

This success was actually a sideline to the Ingoldsbys' main business venture, Tiger Milk (yes, that energy supplement you find in orange-and-black striped cans in health food stores). So as sales grew, they eventually decided to turn the packaging, marketing, and distribution of the rocks over to a small toy company in Chicago and restrict their involvement to the manufacturing of the mix. This way they were able to keep what was in the formula (which had undergone changes since the Undersea Garden was first introduced, but had long been a well-kept secret) to themselves. To placate executives who feared, "What will happen to us if something happens to you?" a copy was signed, sealed, and placed in their attorney's vault for safe keeping. It's still there.

The Way It Works:

The primary ingredients in the Magic Rocks solution are sodium silicate and magnesium sulfate (or Epsom salt). You could easily mix them together on your own—and even get rocks to grow—but you'll only get white rocks. The Ingoldsbys' secret is in the dye, and it's what's in the dye that no one's telling.

No two rocks are alike.

On the average, Magic Rocks will grow from two to four inches tall. Combine two packages and you'll just get more rocks, not bigger rocks.

Magic Rocks were a hip home accessory in the late '50s and early '60s. Decorators used them to create off-beat furnishings, such as lamps and table bases. The biggest assemblage of rocks ever "grown" was for Lou Costello, who had a specially commissioned black and white Magic Rocks garden in the master bedroom of his Hollywood Hills house.

magic slate

THE PLACE: The U.S. Embassy in Moscow.

THE MISSION: A super-sensitive inspection of the new facility.

THE PROBLEM: How do you communicate when chances are good the building has been bugged?

THE ANSWER: Magic Slate.

In fact, prior to a trip to the Soviet Union in the spring of 1987, Representatives Dan Mica (D-Florida) and Olympia Snowe (R-Maine) received strict orders from the State Department to take a dozen of the popular dime-store items with them. The idea worked. Messages could be passed back and forth, then, most importantly, erased with the flick of a wrist.

Guess it shouldn't surprise anyone that it took the Feds over sixty years to notice what kids had always known. What neither of them knew, however, is that if it wasn't for the fact that prostitution is illegal, the Magic Slate might never have come to be.

In the early 1920s, R. A. Watkins, the owner of a small commercial printing plant in Aurora, Illinois, was visited by a man who wanted to sell him the rights to a homemade quick-erase writing device made of waxed cardboard and tissue. The item had potential—as a reusable time sheet or memo pad, for starters—but Watkins, wanting to think it over, asked the man to return in the morning. That night, after the family had gone to bed, the phone rang. It was the inventor, who was calling from jail. The poor guy had been arrested—for soliciting a minor and then taking her across state lines, no less—and told Watkins that if he would bail him out, he would give him the erasable board. Having already decided it was a natural product for his company, Watkins agreed. The man kept his word, handed the prototype over as soon as he was released, and was never heard from again.

In the beginning, Magic Slates were manufactured in a range of sizes and were mainly sold to companies who used them in advertising promotions or as premiums (they did a long stint as a Crackerjacks prize). Although several designs had popular game boards printed on them (such as tic-tac-toe), it wasn't until World War II, when bikes and model trains were in limited production, that the company struck a licensing deal with Disney and heavily marketed the item as a kids' toy.

In one of the more visible downsides to the fall of Communism, Western Publishing, the current owner/maker of Magic Slate (not to mention the publishers of Golden Books), was never awarded a fat government contract, but does—gratis—still send an occasiopal case to the Pentagon.

Former U.S. Congressman Dan Mica in 1987, following his trip to the Soviet Union

matchbox

The corporate veep cruises down the freeway in his luxury sedan. In the lane next to him, a young dad, juggling his '90s sensibilities, drives a four-door utility vehicle and his daughter's soccer team. To his right, a graduate student sneaks sips from the cup of coffee that rests precariously on the dashboard of his ten-year-old hatchback.

What do they—and countless other men behind the wheels of pickups, wagons, vans, convertibles, and coupes—have in common? Studies show that their first car was a Matchbox.

It all dates back to June 19, 1947, when childhood friends with the same last name (Smith) combined their first names (Leslie and Rodney)—and their resources (about $1,000)—to buy a used die-casting machine, lease a bombed-out London building, and start an electrical parts manufacturing firm (Lesney Products). Over the years, to keep the facility operating at full capacity, the company would take advantage of periods of idle time by making and marketing other metal items. In the early '50s, one of these was a 16-inch toy replica of the British Royal State Coach. Response was strong enough that in 1952, when Queen Elizabeth II was crowned, Lesney decided to come out with a smaller and more affordable souvenir version. This time around, over a million units were sold. Realizing

that they were on to something, it wasn't long before the two Smiths decided to dump what they had been doing and convert all production to miniature die-cast cars.

Their third partner, Jack Odell, created the first model: a brass prototype of a small road roller. It was one of a series of four that also included a dumper, a cement mixer, and a tractor. When his daughter asked to take the road roller with her to school, he put it in a tiny carton so she could carry it. And when the line was shown at the Harrogate Toy Fair in 1954 and buyers saw a problem in the fact that cars this little were not packaged, Odell suggested Lesney use the same cardboard container he had given his kid. He described it as being "about the size and shape of a matchbox." Not only did it solve the marketing dilemma, it also gave the new toy line its signature name.

Business jumped with the addition of a red fire engine and the double-decker London bus—two vehicles that kids easily recognized. But it was 1956 when sales showed their biggest jump. For starters, the first sports car (a MG Midget TD) was produced and shortly after that, the entire collection found distribution in the U.S. Let there be little doubt how important this new market was: within months, the formerly all-British fleet included a Ford Customline Station Wagon.

A Superfast series of Matchbox cars was introduced in 1969 to compete with Mattel's Hot Wheels, which had caused Lesney's U.S. sales to dropped from $28 million to $6 million in less than two years. For many collectors, the most desirable models are the ones released before this date, in particular a 1948 Soap Box Racer. Experts say only twenty or so exist today (the original—which never came in a box—was such a poor seller that most were sent back to the distributor and melted down as scrap). In mint condition, it can be worth upwards of $2,000.

The most purchased Matchbox to date has been the NB-38 Model A Van, first issued in 1982. Over time, it has come in multiple variations; the favorite (3 million of this version alone were sold) was the one that had a Kellogg's logo on the side.

mexican jumping beans

When Joy Clement's husband Robert, a candy wholesaler, returned from a business trip to Mexico in 1962, he handed her a pocketful of beans and told her he wanted to start selling them. She told him he had beans for brains. But despite her reluctance, in about a year the two had set up business. And in an era of Instant Fish and Amazing Sea Monkeys, it didn't take long before things were, well, jumping for Joy (and Bob).

From the beginning, their curio/toy was sold three at a time in little plastic boxes. It was a lot of bang for well under a buck. And while it wasn't hard to figure out what these magic beans did, what none of us ever knew was why.

The Way It Works:

Every spring, certain adult moths lay eggs in the flowers of the Yerba de la Flecha trees in the Sonoran desert. The flowers develop into seed pods, encasing the eggs at the same time the eggs are hatching and turning into tiny 3/16-inch caterpillars. The pods fall off the trees (the caterpillars within) and, *voilà*—Mexican Jumping Beans. Simply put, it's the movement of the caterpillar trapped inside that makes the bean jump.

The caterpillar is there, however, because it wants to be. It can breathe since the shell of the pod is porous; the seed serves as its source of food. And eventually (if it makes it this long, since only the strongest do) the caterpillar will poke a pin-size escape hole in the shell and emerge—as a moth. Let it go on record that because it is far away from its home environment, this moth will not lay eggs, will not reproduce, and most important, will not eat holes in clothes.

There's a method to the caterpillar's madness. Jumping patterns have been spotted—enough so that a professor of physiology at the State University of New York in Syracuse uses beans to teach mathematical theory.

Although the average bean is good for 500,000 jumps and might keep jumping for as long as a year, its peak activity period occurs in the first six to eight weeks after it is harvested (usually in early July). While the beans are very sensitive and respond to light, the best way to tell if it's a "live" one is to shake it. If it rattles, it's a dud.

A UPS driver once abandoned his truck and ran for the hills, because, not knowing one of the packages contained jumping beans, he thought he had a rattlesnake on board. And at a terminal in Chicago's O'Hare Airport, passengers were evacuated and explosive experts called in when security mistook a shipment of beans passing through for a ticking bomb.

The monopoly game

For the last six decades, Monopoly, the real estate trading game, has held just what its name implies—and remains the most well-known and best-selling game in the world today.

Traditionally its history has begun with Charles B. Darrow, a Germantown, Pennsylvania, heating engineer. Like a lot of people left unemployed by the Depression, Darrow consoled himself with local homemade games where the rewards were instant wealth and easy money. It was Darrow who submitted his version to Parker Brothers in 1934, though it seems to me he was influenced by others he had played, including The Landlord Game, where players won by buying and selling real estate.

Still, Darrow didn't have it easy. At the end of the initial test session by company executives, the game was unanimously turned down. The reason was that it had "52 fundamental errors," chief among them that it took too long to play, the rules were too complicated, and players went around the board continuously instead of ending up at a final goal. Unfazed, Darrow continued on his own, manufacturing 5,000 copies and selling them to Wannamaker's in Philadelphia. When word of his success got back to Parker Brothers, the company reconsidered and proceeded to buy the rights.

The Monopoly game is published in forty countries (generally translated into foreign real estate and currency) and printed in twenty-five languages, including Croatian and Icelandic. There has been a braille edition, a completely edible chocolate version, a set made by Alfred Dunhill that included silver houses and gold hotels (and sold for $25,000), a life-size reproduction (at Juniata College in Huntington, Pennsylvania), and a laminated steel-backed board so scuba divers could play underwater. Additionally, since 1994, Parker Brothers has licensed USAopoly, authorized editions of the Monopoly game where the rules, token, and money are the same, but the real estate is changed to reflect buildings and businesses in Boston, New York, San Francisco, Atlanta, or San Diego, instead of Atlantic City.
All pretty impressive for a product that George Parker himself not only called a fad, but predicted would last no more than three years on the market. In fact, in December 1936, he ordered that his company cease making any more boards or utensil boxes. But sales continued—even rose—and Parker happily admitted his mistake.

The Monopoly game was one of many games prisoners were allowed in their cells at the Faulkner County Jail in Arkansas (Guess you can't get too bummed out over having to "Go directly to jail" when you're already there). All that changed in November 1994, when three inmates used the wheelbarrow token to remove the tamper-resistant screws on air duct coverings, then crawled their way through the ducts and escaped.

The total amount of money in a standard Monopoly game is $15,140.

Real money was slipped into the packs of play money in sets that were smuggled into POW camps inside Germany during WW II.

Marvin Gardens is the only property on the board not named after a street. In actuality it is an upscale area composed of Margate City and Ventor City which, had it been spelled correctly, should have been Marven Gardens.

In 1972, when Atlantic City was undergoing extensive urban renewal, plans were in effect to change the names of Baltic and Mediterranean Avenues to Fairmont and Melrose until hundreds of Monopoly game fans showed up to voice their protest at a public hearing and the measure was defeated.

In all these years there have been only a few minor variations in the game: While every set comes with ten metal tokens, a total of twenty different objects have been cast over time, so the playing pieces alternate. And although the houses and hotels were originally made of wood, Parker Brothers switched to plastic in 1958.

The Monopoly Man, aka Rich Uncle Milburn Pennybags, made his first appearance the second year the game was on the market.

mr. potato head

They convinced us to always wear clean underwear and scared us into thinking that if we crossed our eyes too much they might get stuck that way. But hard as they may have tried, our parents could never get us to stop playing with our food.

It's probably a good bet that the kids of George Lerner also liked to play with their food. Only somewhere along the line, he had the insight to turn their poor manners into profits. Lerner was a model maker, well known in the toy industry. In 1950 he molded a set of sharp-pronged plastic pieces—shaped like eyes, ears, noses, and mouths—that could be stuck into fruits or vegetables (in particular, potatoes) to create a range of funny faces. After pedaling this novelty item unsuccessfully for several years, he finally sold it to a breakfast food company. What they planned to do was to package a handful of the pieces in a bag, then offer them as premiums in boxes of cereal; what they offered to pay George Lerner was $5,000.

It was a fair deal, but it could have cost him millions. That's because several months later Lerner had a meeting with Henry and Merrill Hassenfeld, the father and son team who operated Hasbro Industries. Known at the time for making play doctors' and nurses' kits, the company was looking to expand; one look at the funny face set and they felt certain that this was the item with which to do it. Except for one small obstacle: Lerner no longer owned the rights. Lucky for him, Hasbro didn't let it drop, and eventually Merrill Hassenfeld reached an agreement where his company would pay the cereal company $2,000 to stop production on the premium.

The Mr. Potato Head toy was the first toy to ever be advertised on television. The pitch was simple and to the point: "Meet Mr. Potato Head, the most wonderful friend a boy or girl could have." Millions of kids agreed.

Adam had Eve, Ike had Mamie, and with his great success that first year, Mr. Potato Head got a wife. Actually, he got an entire family, including not only Mrs. Potato Head, but—if your parents splurged for the super deluxe set— son Spud and daughter Yam.

In 1987, with anti-smoking campaigns in full swing, Hasbro announced, after thirty-five years, that it was no longer packaging Mr. Potato Head with his signature pipe. A big deal was made of his decision to quit and the last pipe was handed over to Surgeon General C. Everett Coop at a press conference for the Great American Smokeout.

The Evolution of a Toy Tuber:

Phase 1. Since first introduced in May 1952—when he came boxed as a mix of twenty-eight different face pieces and accessories—Mr. Potato Head has gone through some pretty major changes.

Phase 2. The original concept of using actual fruits and vegetables was dropped in 1964, when Hasbro began supplying a plastic potato with each kit. (The advent of plastic potatoes led to other plastic food and it wasn't long before Cooky the Cucumber, Oscar the Orange, Katie the Carrot, and Pete the Pepper came boxed with Mr. Potato Head as "his Tooty Frooty Friends"—an odd choice for a name, by the way, since three of the four were vegetables. They were followed two years later by the lesser-remembered Picnic Pals: Frenchy Fry, Franky Frank, and Willy Burger, as well as Mr. Soda Pop Head, Mr. Mustard Head, and Mr. Ketchup Head. What was unique about these six is that many of their face pieces were also food-influenced: ears were halved-sliced onions; mouths were made to look like baby gherkins.) Newly passed U.S. safety standards required that the prongs on the face pieces be less sharp (once revised, they were unable to puncture real food). And a lot of kids (trying to be good and picking up their toys) had not only been putting the pieces back into the box when they were done, but also, the potato. Needless to say, over time, this created quite a stink.

Phase 3. But starting in the late '70s—and continuing through today—Mr. Potato Head has become virtually unrecognizable to the nostalgic eye. His head and body are now one piece, face parts are a good five times larger their original size (a result of more stringent safety regulations), and his derby hat and sensible shoes have been ditched in favor of a baseball cap and sneakers (Yo! Tater Man!). None of this has stopped kids from loving—and wanting—him; it's their parents who are shocked when they first see their old friend after a long time.

N E R F ball

Hot on the heels of his success with Twister (see page 39), Reyn Guyer said bye-bye to the sales promotion business and started another company that—no big surprise—specialized in developing new toys. Around 1968, one product his team was putting together was a caveman game that included rocks carved out of

foam rubber as playing pieces. While trying to make it work, Guyer smoothed and shaped the foam with scissors, until eventually it took the shape of a ball.

Clearly, even though accidently, he was on to something: a foam ball was a great idea if for no other reason than you could throw it without fear of hurting or breaking something. Still, group consensus was that the ball, on its own, would get lost on the toy store shelves. So Guyer and staff incorporated it into various games sets—for volleyball, basketball, baseball, and anything else they could think of that traditionally involved a circular ball. The hook, of course, was that all of these outdoor favorites could now be played indoors. But after showing the mock-ups to Parker Brothers, a funny thing happened. The game giant loved the foam idea; it's just what they wanted—all they wanted was the 4-inch ball.

In the next few months, several names—including Moon, Muff, and Falsie—were tossed around until executives settled on introducing "the first official indoor ball" as the Nerf.

Nerf Balls were taken aboard the space shuttle Endeavor and used by astronauts to help investigate the effects of gravity; Nerf airplanes played a part in a training program for avoiding midair collisions run by the U.S. Air Force; and a Nerf football was key to the rehabilitation therapy set up for 49er quarterback Steve Young when he injured the thumb on his throwing hand.

All Nerf balls—along with the forty-one other Nerf brand products—are made by cutting huge chunks of dense foam with a hot wire.

Not only is the Nerf football the most popular item in the product line, it is the largest-selling football in the world.

The prototype for the Nerf Ball was hand cut from yellow foam, then spray-painted orange. Every year, it is hauled out from safekeeping and used as an ornament on the Guyer family Christmas tree.

PEZ

When it comes to kid stuff, Pez stands alone.

No other product combines the two greatest pleasures of childhood—toys and candy—and does it all in a permanent plastic package that could possibly be even *more* popular than the licensed characters it depicts.

It's a marketing success story, and of course, none of it was planned. Back in Austria in 1927, Eduard Haas III (who had already made a fortune in baking powder and dessert mixes) combined peppermint oil with sugar, and compressed the concoction into tiny brick-shaped tablets that he stacked, wrapped, and wholesaled as a high-quality breath mint. In search for a name, he simply abbreviated the German word *pfefferminz* (meaning peppermint) and called his newest product Pez.

Over the years, a big part of Pez's popularity was as a substitute for smoking, so in response, Haas created a dispenser. Cleverly designed to resemble a cigarette lighter, it also functioned like one. Which meant it could be operated with one hand, and pressing down with your thumb on a lever caused the top to tilt back and a single mint to pop out.

A proven hit in Europe, Pez came to America in 1952. Only breath candies—particularly intense peppermint ones—didn't really cut it here and the product quickly fizzled. Not that that stopped Haas. Following a little market research, he simply changed the formula to fruit flavors, started manufacturing the tablets in colors (to match their new tastes), and decided to reposition the dispenser as a kids' item by adding a molded, three-dimensional cartoon head on top. According to some stories, his first one was Mickey Mouse; others remember it as Popeye. Whichever it was, it was brilliant.

It's hard to calculate how many heads have been cast since then (company officials will only say "hundreds and hundreds" because over the last forty years, there have been different versions of the same character and in some cases even the same version has come in multiple color variations), but between thirty and forty are on the market at any given time. The majority of them are licensed characters, balanced out by a handful of original creations (usually seasonal dispensers, like Santa Claus, the Easter Bunny, or a Halloween witch). With a costly design process and a production schedule that can take about a year, the list reads like a who's who of the cartoon world, as the company strives to avoid passing fads (so no Alf) and steers away from movie tie-ins (a lesson they learned with *Annie*). Never have they depicted a real person

(despite repeated requests for Elvis), nor will they start. For two main reasons: rarely do real people have interestingly shaped heads, and all too frequently, they wind up in the middle of a front-page scandal not particularly in keeping with their status as a kids' toy.

Although always intended to be collected (you got one, you wanted more), it is only since the late '80s that Pez has become a sought-after collectible. Among the more unsual: the full-figure Santa Claus (where instead of the traditional rectangle, the dispenser is shaped like Santa's body); the soft-headed monsters; the Pez gun; and the "Make-a-Face," which came with an oversized blank head and eighteen miniature face pieces, a sort of Pez meets Mr. Potato Head.
But the best proof of Pez's popularity is the story of one entrepreneur who created a display stand for dispensers, only in doing so, reproduced the name PEZ on his product without the company's permission. Hit with a 'cease and desist' letter from the executive offices in Connecticut, he framed the correspondence—then promptly sold it to another collector for $300.

Three faces of Mickey
(left to right) late 1950s, early 1970s, and today

Despite an internal overhaul (which saw the metal spring mechanism replaced with an irremovable plastic piece) in order to childproof the dispenser, the major visible change in Pez happened in the mid-1980s when "feet" were added so that the figure could stand up more easily.

While the dispensers are made overseas (with different characters, for obvious reasons, created for different countries), since 1973, the candy for American Pez (currently lemon, orange, strawberry, and grape) has come from the Pez factory in Connecticut. Grape replaced cherry in the early '80s, when company executives decided that they didn't need two "red" flavors and acknowledged that cherry conjured up memories of medicine and cough syrup. Past Pez have also ranged from choco-late to apple; present day special orders have included sugar-free and Kosher.

One of the largest public displays of Pez dispensers can be found in Burlingame, California, at the Museum of Pez Memorabilia. Housed in a 20'x80' room at the rear of a computer store, the museum doesn't charge admission. Guided tours are available with reservations and the gift shop features an extensive stock of Pez both past and present. 214 California Drive, Burlingame, California. (415)347-4576.

play-doh

brand modeling compound

Joe McVicker was working for his father's firm, a Cincinnati manufacturer of soaps and cleaning products, and probably could have spent the rest of his life doing just that if one thing hadn't gotten in the way: by the time he was twenty-seven, McVicker had become a millionaire.

All because his sister-in-law, a New Jersey teacher, casually mentioned that the modeling clay supplied to her nursery school class was too firm for her students' small fingers to manipulate. Her complaint made Joe wonder if he in fact didn't have the answer—in the form of non-toxic compound (a pliant putty-like substance that was not only easily malleable, but stayed soft indefinitely if kept in a tightly sealed container) that he had formulated (and had been selling) to clean wallpaper. After a series of tests to double-check that it was safe, he mailed off some samples to her school, where it got high marks from both the faculty and the kids.

Curious to see if he could take this venture further, McVicker met with the Cincinnati Board of Education, who agreed to buy the product for all the kindergartens and elementary schools in their area. Next it was showcased at a big educational convention, where it was seen by the wife of a buyer for Woodward & Lothrop in Washington, D.C. From that came a successful in-store demo; then word of mouth led to orders from other major retailers such as Macy's and Marshall Field. By 1956, the wallpaper cleaner-turned-kids' toy had become known as "Play-Doh brand, the original reusable modeling compound," and the name (and nature) of the family business changed from Kutol Chemicals to Rainbow Crafts.

Beyond playgrounds and playrooms, Play-Doh has squeezed its way into a range of artists' studios, where it has been molded into everything from architectural models of famous buildings (such as Monticello, which was assembled from 2,500 miniature handmade bricks) to Walter Williams's popular *Saturday Night Live* character Mr. Bill.

Despite the new name (Rainbow), Play-Doh brand modeling compound was only available in off-white until its second year on the market, when company chemist Dr. Tien Liu concocted red, blue, and yellow colors (along with a newer, softer consistency). The product's palette got a second boost in the early 1980s; it was then that purple, green, orange, and pink were added to the mix. Day-glo and glitter variations later followed.

In a heavily proprietary industry, the formula for Play-Doh brand modeling compound is probably the toy world's best kept secret, although it's a common belief that the ingredient which gives the product its distinct smell is vanilla.

September 16 has officially been declared National Play-Doh Day.

R A D I O

flyer

At the age of fifteen, Antonio Pasin left his native Italy and came to the United States in search of opportunity. Less than a year later, in 1917, he found it. It did not come while he was working in a piano factory or for a cabinet maker (he did both), but on his own, in the form of wooden wagons he would craft at night and sell to Chicago-area hardware stores during the day. Rather than constructing a miniature version to use as a product sample, Pasin preferred to show off the real thing, so he carted his creation around in pieces, which he would pull from a battered suitcase and then assemble in front of potential buyers. His plan worked; business steadily grew, and in 1923 he founded the Liberty Coaster Company, a name he chose to honor his new homeland.

Within two years, Pasin had not only made his fortune, he had sold the business, returned to Italy and married. By the late 1920s, however, he was back—to buy back the company he had created (which was struggling to survive the Depression), and to introduce a second wagon that would change childhood forever.

What was so different is that, intrigued by the new, cutting-edge technology used to make cars, Pasin fashioned this particular model out of metal—a scrap piece of automobile steel to be exact. Once finished, he painted it red, then stenciled the words "Radio Flyer" in white letters on the side. "Flyer," because it connoted motion; "Radio" in honor of another revolutionary item that had also been invented by an Italian.

Liberty was renamed Radio Steel & Manufacturing in 1930, then became known as Radio Flyer in 1987. Over the years, the original design has been made safer, sleeker, bigger (including the popular Radio Rancher in the late 1950s), smaller, yet has never gone out of style. Kids still spend hours loading and unloading it, hauling around their treasures or climbing aboard so they can be taken for a ride. The rich red color still remains. As does the signature silhouette of the "boy on the wagon," which even in these days of mass production is still stenciled on by hand.

Without a doubt, the most elaborate—and most unique—Radio Flyer was introduced in the mid-1930s and was known as the Streak-O-Lite Deluxe. Ivory with red accents, it had deco-style detailing and came equipped with headlights, horn, spoke wheels, and a dashboard instrument panel that looked "just like Dad's."

The story has all the makings of a three-hankie movie—a dying child, a doting father, and the simple plaything that bonded them together. While there's a good deal of truth in the retelling, no doubt the dramatic details have been embellished over time. But chances are it happened like this:

raggedy ann

In 1906, Johnny Gruelle's daughter Marcella found a worn rag doll in the attic of her grandmother's home. With her parents' help, she patched and restuffed it; then Gruelle—a newspaper cartoonist and illustrator—painted on a new face, distinguishing it with a unique triangular nose. Together, they named their creation Raggedy Ann, a combination of the title characters *(The Raggedy Man and Little Orphan Annie)* from two favorite poems by family friend James Witcomb Riley.

In making up Raggedy Ann stories to entertain Marcella, Gruelle quickly realized the character's potential, which could explain why a floppy rag doll (usually dangling from a kid's hand) started to appear in his comic strip "Mr. Twee Deedle." It definitely explains why he secured a patent and a trademark for his design in 1915, and even began handcrafting a small quantity of dolls (one interesting difference: the yarn hair was brown, not red) to sell. During all this, Marcella became terminally ill, the result of a contaminated smallpox vaccination. It was to cope with her death—and to assure that in some way his daughter lived on—that Gruelle wrote and illustrated the *Raggedy Ann Stories*, a compilation of all the tales he had told to her over the years. Perhaps as significant as the book's release in early 1918 is the fact that several months later the Volland company followed up with a commercially manufactured Raggedy Ann doll, making her possibly the first—but unarguably the longest-running—character license in the toy industry.

She's been called a doll with heart, and for good reason: every Raggedy Ann actually has one. Most of these hearts have been silk-screened on, but the Gruelles' homemade Anns supposedly had a heart-shaped candy (imprinted with "I Love You") sewn inside, while the first mass-produced Volland version contained a die-cut cardboard heart. It couldn't be seen, but it could be felt, if you ran your fingers across the chest.

The dolls have had an interesting manufacturing history with no less than a half dozen different companies responsible for their production at various times. The rarest (and hence, the most valuable) may be the dolls put out by the Exposition Company in the mid-1930s (due to competition from a cheap knockoff that glutted the marketplace, fewer of these were made; as a result, only ten are known to exist today). The oddest came from Georgene Novelties and had blue vertical (as opposed to red horizontal) stripes on the legs (so much for quality control). And the most remembered (which probably makes them the most popular) are either the later Georgenes from the '50s or the Knickerbocker Raggedys from the '60s, since both were a Baby Boomer basic.

Although constantly overshadowed by the higher-profile Barbie, Raggedy Ann is definitely a player, with her own newsletter (*Rags*), her own store (The Last Great Co., in Cashiers, North Carolina), and even her own festival, held annually the weekend preceding Memorial Day weekend in Arcola, Illinois—the birthplace of Johnny Gruelle. *The Raggedy Ann & Andy Festival/Arcola Chamber of Commerce; (217) 268-4530.*

Ready-to-fly
BALSA PLANES

U.S. Navy Ensign Paul Guillow had just gotten out of the service when, drawing on his own experience as a World War I fighter pilot, he decided to capitalize on the country's interest in flight (thank you, Charles Lindberg) and market a card game called "Lucky Lady." His product took off, only to be quickly knocked off by a leading toy manufacturer. Realizing that he would never be able to compete, Guillow shifted the focus of his business and began offering model kits with which miniature versions of historic aircrafts could be replicated out of balsa wood.

For kids, constructing one was a complicated process: first patterns had to be traced, then the individual pieces cut out using an X-acto knife (if you didn't slip and slice the wood, chances were good you sliced your finger). After that, the whole thng had to be assembled—only cement glue would do and it was best applied with the tip of a toothpick. More often than not, a plane took weeks—not to mention Dad's help—to finish. But things got easier (and sales soared higher) when Guillow introduced a "ready-to-fly" line in the early 1940s. Not only were these inexpensive, they required no more know-how than slipping a one-piece wing through a pre-fab body. And while all were launched by hand, the most popular had the added power of a rubber band engine that you wound by turning the propeller. The hardest part was winding it tight—yet not too tight that the band would break—then keeping it from unwinding before you had the chance to get it airborne. Sure, any balsa wood plane thrown into the air could glide, but the magic of this one was that it actually *flew.*

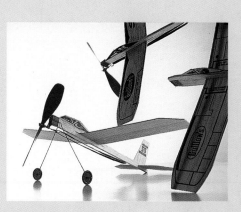

Despite their popularity, Guillow's airplanes almost disappeared during the 1940s (in fact, what was on the market was made of foam), because balsa wood—needed for life rafts aboard naval vessels—was unavailable for civilian use throughout World War II.

Balsa wood is a natural crop that is harvested solely in Ecuador. Though it grows like crabgrass, it takes seven years to mature, eventually reaching heights of 60 feet and diameters of 12 inches.

roadmaster

TRICYCLE

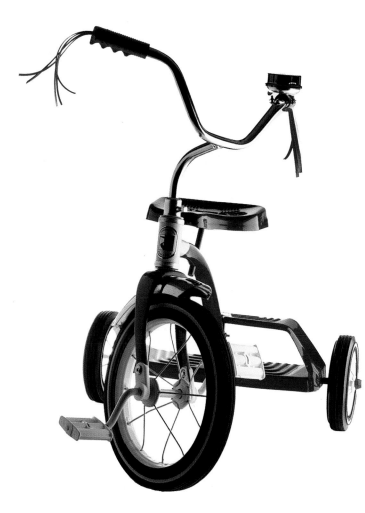

To a kid, life could seem intolerable. Limited freedom, parental demands, siblings ready to tattle at every turn. So naturally, we longed for the moment we could escape it all. And for most of us, independence first came in the form of a candy apple red three-wheeler with whitewall tires and touches of chrome.

While Roadmaster (or The Junior Toy Company, the firm it bought out) can't be credited with inventing the tricycle, they certainly perfected it—although not without our help. We added bells and buzzers and clown-like horns, hung plastic streamers from the handgrips and attached playing cards to hit the spokes and mimic motor-cycle sounds. Perched atop the seat, insurmountable distances—down the drive, across the street, to the top of a hill—were now reduced to nothing. Pedaling faster blurred our problems obsolete, and increased momentum gave us power. On our bikes, the world was our oyster.

At least until Mom called us to come in.

the new Sky Trike

No. 885 SERIES Sky Trike TUBULAR VELOCIPEDES
Three Sizes

Knuckle Guards and Streamer Grips   1.75" Semi-Pneumatic Molded Tires
New Junior Jet Design Handlebar   Chrome Plated Truss Rods and Fender Shields

A Roadmaster tricycle as offered in 1954 (above) and a Roadmaster today (left).

S I L L Y
putty

It probably shouldn't come as a surprise: You earn your success as the life of the party so no one believes you started out doing serious work. But often—as in this case—it's true.

When the Japanese invasion of the Far East during World War II cut off the United States' rubber supply (hence threatening mass production of much-needed tires and boots), the government's War Protection Board asked General Electric to develop an inexpensive synthetic substitute. At the company's lab in New Haven, James Wright, a chemical engineer working on the project, experimented with boric acid and silicone oil. The two substances unexpectedly gelled, resulting in a gooey compound, which (when tossed on the floor) didn't just bounce back—it bounced better and higher than rubber. It also stretched farther, withstood decay longer, and had the bizarre ability to lift images off the pages of a newspaper or comic book. Interesting stuff; the problem was that neither Wright nor any other prominent engineer to whom GE sent a sample could find a practical use for it.

So Wright's "bouncing putty" became a curiosity of New Haven business and science circles and started making the rounds at cocktail parties, where its ability to amuse guests caught the attention of Ruth Fallgatter (a toy store owner) and Peter Hodgson (the marketing consultant contracted to produce her holiday catalog).

Together, they decided to include Bouncing Putty on a page spotlighting novelty gifts for adults. There was no product picture, only a simple description; an ounce, offered in a clear plastic case, sold for two dollars.

And sold better than anything else in the catalog (save a 50-cent box of Crayolas). Still, Fallgatter had no interest in further marketing the product, but Hodgson, already $12,000 in debt, knew he couldn't afford to let it drop. He borrowed money, purchased a huge batch of the putty from GE (for $147), then hired students (from Yale, no less) to separate it into one-ounce balls (which they packaged in multicolored plastic eggs). Since "bouncing" only described one of the multiple things this substance could do, he changed the name to one which better reflected what he was selling: Silly Putty.

Attending the New York Toy Fair in 1950, Hodgson did not have great success (in fact, he was urged to quit while he was ahead), but he did manage to sign a few accounts, including the Doubleday bookshops. Although he didn't know it at the time, that was all he needed. Six months later a staff writer for *The New Yorker* would discover it at one of the chain's Manhattan stores, mention it in the magazine's popular "Talk of the Town" column, and in three days, Hodgson's orders would top a quarter of a million. To date, more than 200 million eggs of Silly Putty have been sold.

Over the years, Silly Putty hasn't really changed, but the process used to print most color comics has, greatly limiting its ability to lift images off the pages of the Sunday funnies.

While originally only available in peach, fluorescent shades of Silly Putty were added in 1990, with a glow-in-the-dark version introduced the following year.

Despite scientists' claim that it had no practical application, Silly Putty has been used by everyone from pilots (as ear plugs) and secretaries (to clean typewriter keys) to athletes (who squeeze it to strengthen their grip), dry cleaners (as a method to remove lint from clothing), and restaurateurs (beats a matchbook for leveling the legs of a wobbly table). It has also found its way into outer space (where it was carried aboard Apollo 8 to keep tools fastened down during weightlessness), into the Columbus Zoo (as a means of casting gorilla footprints needed for identification records), and into several contemporary galleries (thanks to New York artist George Horner, who utilizes it as his canvas in collages that are a mix of folk art, funk and fun). *George Horner (718) 857-1140.*

NOTHING ELSE IS
Silly Putty®
Silly Putty
THE REAL SOLID LIQUID

Slinky

In 1943, Richard James, a marine engineer at Philadelphia's Cramp Shipyard, was working on a meter designed to monitor horsepower on naval battleships. As he struggled to formulate an inner spring that would assure that the machine, even if rocked at sea, could give an accurate reading, he mistakenly knocked one of the prototypes he had developed (and subsequently rejected) off his desk. Oddly, the spring didn't just fall to the ground and land; instead, after it hit, it spiraled—coil by coil, end over end—across the office floor.

This unexpected response intrigued James, but his interest had nothing to do with how it might affect the project he had been assigned. That evening he took his discovery home, showed it to his wife Betty and announced his plan—to turn it into a toy. While he tested various metals, thicknesses, and proportions to perfect it, she combed the dictionary in search of the perfect name. What she came up with was Slinky. Borrowing $500, the Jameses had a small quantity of these springs manufactured, then set out to sell them through local retail outlets. But despite the toy's amazing ability to walk, it didn't move. Reasoning that the product had no name recognition and people needed to be shown what it could do, the couple convinced Gimbels to let them set up an in-store demonstration. Smart thinking. One glance at this fat steel coil as it gracefully crawled down a sloped board and within minutes, the entire stock of 400 had been sold. Fifty years and 250 million Slinkys later, Betty James still runs the company she started with her husband in 1946.

One standard-sized Slinky contains 80 feet of wire.

The final product may look like a simple spiral, but it is actually so intricate that when Xerox had trouble fabricating a coiled spring needed for a new product, they had the work done at the Slinky factory.

Aside from a junior version (and one made of colored plastic), the Slinky has remained virtually unchanged, although the wire is now coated for durability and its ends have been crimped for safety.

The Slinky song (It's Slinky, it's Slinky/for fun it's a won-der-ful toy/It's Slinky, it's Slinky/it's fun for a girl and a boy) has been used in the company's TV commercials continuously since 1962, making it the longest-running jingle in advertising history.

Z-Axis, a North Carolina design firm, has stretched a Slinky around a cylindrical polycarbonate lamp shade to create a contemporary lighting fixture stylish enough to be featured in The Whitney Museum. Additionally, Slinkys have been incorporated into devices designed to pick pecans from trees, have doubled as pigeon repellers and gutter protectors, have served as makeshift radio antennas (by U.S. troops in Vietnam), and, in an ironic return to their roots, have been taken aboard ships and implemented to help counterbalance wave motion.

SNEEZING POWDER

WHOOPEE CUSHIONS

and other

NOVELTY GAGS

While working for a New Jersey firm that marketed coal by-products, Sam Adams was intrigued by one chemical that the company had trouble moving because whenever customers came in contact with it, they sneezed. In fact, so potent was this substance that just a little, placed in the palm of someone's hand and blown randomly into the air, could make an entire *roomful* of people start sneezing. Although his boss had no interest in the stuff, Adams tried the powder out on unsuspecting friends, quickly realizing that its inherent problem was also its biggest asset. Always the opportunist (we're talking about a guy who'd been a pool shark at the ripe old age of twelve), he offered to buy out the remaining stock. He then put the powder into individual packets, gave it a catchy name (Cachoo) and started selling it.

A Philadelphia retailer ordered 70,000 Cachoos, which might explain how it got widely circulated at the 1908 political conventions. But soon other companies began knocking him off (not to mention undercutting him), and Adams realized that if he was going to survive in the practical joke business, he had to stay one punchline ahead. Hence, his second important contribution to American culture. It was extracted from a weed in India that was legendary for making any horse or cow who walked through it scratch like crazy. Itching Powder.

Stink bombs came next. Then dribble glasses and squirting flowers. Everywhere Adams turned, he saw a possible gag (over time, he would invent 700 of them). For the classic snakes-in-a-nuts can, he only had to look as far as across the kitchen table. He had noticed how every morning after breakfast, when he went to put the jam jar away, his wife would remind him to be sure he clamped the lid on tightly, and then, disbelieving that he had, would double-check to see for herself. Tired of being treated like a child, he decided to teach her a lesson. First, he covered a three-foot coil of wire with a piece of skin-like cloth, then compressed it into an empty six-inch jam jar, securing it with the lid. The idea was that when his wife went to check on him and lifted off the top, this giant "snake" would jump out and scare her. It did—and it worked so well that soon it was added to the company's inventory.

But the premiere prank in the S. S. Adams product line is, without a doubt, the Joy Buzzer, that windup device that tickles the other person's palm when they shake your hand. Though several buzzers had come before his, their large size—one inch by four inches—made it impossible to completely conceal them. Adams's determination took him to Europe, where in 1928 he tracked down a noted German tool and die maker who was able to reduce the mechanism to just one-quarter of an inch thick. His perfectionism paid off: the Joy Buzzer was a major reason the company survived the Depression; it was fun and inexpensive, and the type of thing people needed to help them forget their troubles.

Despite his track record, Adams did, on occasion, blow it big time. And probably no more so than the day in 1930 when he turned down a circular latex pillow sent in from a Toronto rubber manufacturer— one that made a distinctly recognizable sound when sat upon. Owning up to his mistake, within a year the company catalog featured what they called a "Razzberry Cushion." Sixtysome years later, you can still get it, along with seventy-three other time-proven crowd pleasers. Remember disappearing ink? Hot pepper gum? The plastic ice cube with a bug in it? They're all here; proof positive that he who laughs, lasts.

The die maker who revolutionized the Joy Buzzer was a Jewish craftsman who planned to use the money to escape with his family from Nazi Germany. Sadly, after he finished the job, he never showed up to collect his final payment and Adams never heard from him again.

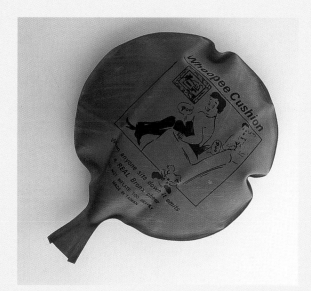

Maurice Chevalier was a big fan of the Joy Buzzer and reportedly had one on hand when he met Tallulah Bankhead while they were both making movies for Paramount in the 1930s. Another satisfied customer was former President George Bush, who not only carried one with him on the campaign trail, but used it to break the ice when meeting bigwigs in tense surroundings.

By the early 1940s the FDA banned the selling of the principal ingredients in both Cachoo and Itching Powder, due to their toxic nature. While Adams had to drop the latter from the line, the former was reformulated. What you'll find on the market today is safe, organic (the main ingredient is pepper) and, as to be expected, nowhere near as potent.

Believe it or not, in the late 1980s, there was actually a worldwide whoopee cushion shortage. Chalk it up to safe sex, and the fact that nowadays the cushions are made by factories in the Far East. Since those same rubber manufacturers had to devote their entire work force to the production of surgical gloves and condoms in order to meet the increased demand created by the AIDS crisis, for approximately two years, there was no time left for making whoopees.

spirograph

Probably aware that kids who love to draw tend to stop the minute they begin to feel they aren't very good at it, Englishman Dennis Fischer drew on his own background as a mechanical engineer and came up with an art toy where success was foolproof and "a million marvelous patterns" guaranteed. It involved pinning down a piece of paper underneath a plastic ring, then manipulating any of a number of interlocking wheels in or around it using the point of a pen. His invention was unique because creating these graphics and designs was a challenge (with unbelievably slick results), yet, amazingly, anyone could do it.

Introduced in Europe at the 1965 Nuremburg International Toy Fair, the product—which Fischer had named Spirograph—was spotted by the executives at Kenner, who quickly snatched up the American rights. But while anticipating success, even they were unprepared for what was to happen next: By 1967, 5.5 million sets had been sold, making it the number one toy in the country for two years in a row. A Spirotot followed, then Spiroman (who, thanks to a pen-dulum that swung from his hand, could do the drawing for you).

Today, Spirograph is one of the few mainstream toys that has crossed over to the classroom. Because it both rewards practice and strengthens use of visual-motor skills, it has established itself as a valuable tool for teachers working with learning- and physically-disabled kids.

BAND SAW

The second decade of this century not only marked the start of a building boom in the United States, but, fittingly, became a heyday for architectural toys.

tinkertoy

Multi-part construction kits were all the rage with kids, and the skyscrapers, windmills, and carousels they first had the chance to make with metal (see Erector Set, page 29), a year later, they were creating out of wood.

The man responsible was, ironically, a stonemason from Evanston, Illinois. Bored with the family business—which boiled down to designing and selling

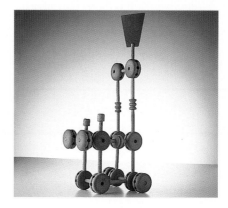

tombstones—Charles Pajeau decided to try his hand at toy making when he noticed how much fun his own children had sticking pencils into empty spools of thread, then haphazardly assembling them into all sorts of abstract forms. Instead of the traditional cylindrical shape, he crafted a shorter, wheel-like spool, with one hole drilled through the center and a series of holes running along the edge (making it possible to build at angles as well as connect multiple dowels at once).

Pajeau and his partner Robert Petit, a stockbroker at the Chicago Board of Trade, called themselves The Toy Tinkers, and their initial product—a cannister of basic wooden parts and pieces that was touted as the "Thousand Wonder Builder"—became known as Tinkertoy.

Timing, however, wasn't in their favor. Despite the success enjoyed by Erector and the fact that their toy appealed to girls as well as boys, it was already June and the marketplace was saturated. Refusing—as the distributors insisted—to wait another year, the pair bypassed the overstocked toy outlets, and took the product (on their own) directly to Chicago-area pharmacies, newspaper stands, and cigar stores. With each deal they made, Pajeau would not only deliver the goods, but also set up an elaborate display, filling the shop windows with models of all types, then installing an electric fan so they would move. Response was so great that even on a limited local level, demand outstripped supply.

Given that success, the Toy Tinkers were surprised by the lukewarm reception they received at the New York Toy Fair the following February. Determined to be recognized, Pajeau relied on a proven formula. As he had in Chicago, he mounted a display, this time in the pharmacy at Grand Central Station. But instead of showcasing a multitude of wind-powered, pre-constructed models, he hired little people, dressed them in Pierrot costumes, and

stood them in the window facing 42nd Street. The sight of these playful characters building huge configurations out of Tinkertoy construction systems caused massive traffic jams, and generated nonstop media attention. Within days, orders had poured in, and by the time the holidays rolled around, the company had produced and shipped close to a million sets.

Millions of Tinkertoys are still sold every year, although there have been noticeable changes. Color came first: originally made of unpainted wood, red sticks were introduced in 1953, then green, yellow, and blue ones were added to the mix in 1955. Since 1992, a major redesign has been in effect. Spools and sticks are not only bigger and longer; they are now made entirely of plastic.

Lockheed has used Tinkertoy construction systems as a design model to test airplane wing and fuselage systems, while Indiana Bell frequently relies on them to gauge the skills of management candidates. Additionally, they are considered a reflection of the development of modern architecture, and are part of the permanent collection of a number of noted museums, including Philadelphia's Franklin Institute of Science (which since 1978 has played host to Tinkertoy Weekends) and the Canadian Centre for Architecture in Montreal (where they proudly share shelf space with Erector Sets and Lincoln Logs).

tonka

WHEN LYNN BAKER, AVERY CROUNSE, AND ALVIN TESCH FOUNDED MOUND METALCRAFT

in the basement of a Minnesota schoolhouse in 1946, it was for the purpose of starting their own business

to manufacture garden instruments (such as hoes, rakes, and shovels) and display fixtures for stores

(including tie, hat, and shoe racks). Toy production was never a part of the plan and, in fact, only entered

the picture because amid the tooling the three men acquired when they purchased a smaller competitor

was a miniature metal Steam Shovel. Although this particular vehicle had not been successful, the trio

began to think that there was possibility in the market for durable, affordable, and realistic toy trucks and

with careful refining, they just might tap into it.

Little did they know. From the beginning, the Steam Shovel (molded out of steel and now with working

parts), as well as a second model (a Crane & Clam), sold better and faster than anything else the com-

pany was manufacturing. So it didn't take long for Baker, Crounse, and Tesch to shift the focus of their

business. To set the new line apart, they named it Tonka Toys (after nearby Lake Minnetonka), added

forklifts, wreckers, and semis, and gave each vehicle a signature logo (of waves and birds) to represent

the area where they were made.

How They Do It:

Although today's trucks contain a great deal more plastic and a lot less steel, the process utilized to create them has changed very little. Each new Tonka begins as a sketch; if favorably received in a consumer test group, it is translated into a three-dimensional clay model. Once that gets the company okay, it is duplicated in metal (sometimes fiberglass), then examined and reviewed for safety. Next, it goes back to the drawing board, where a detailed engineering blueprint is prepared, which leads to yet another sample (this one based on the revised specifications) and more testing (this time by kids). When (and if) the prototype survives this round, the design is finally put into mass production.

To date, the best-selling Tonka brand equipment (over 18 million of this model alone) is the yellow Mighty Dump, introduced in 1964. Often remembered for other reasons is the cherry-red Fire Engine (first manufactured in 1956), which came with a small hydrant through which you could actually hook up to the garden hose. The model was discontinued in 1964 when parents complained that kids were starting real fires in order to put it to the test. But perhaps most desirable among Tonka collectors are the "private labels." These special orders of a standard semi came with the logo or name of a particular client decaled on the side (like Minute Maid, Ace Hardware, or United Van Lines), were neither featured in nor sold through company catalogs, and had a lower-than-average production run (figure 5 to 10,000 pieces). All of which makes them highly sought after, harder to find, and incredibly valuable today.

The word *Tonka* also means "great" in Dakota Sioux, the language of the American Indian tribe native to Minnesota.

VIEW-MASTER

Visiting the Oregon Caves in the summer of 1938, William Gruber, a piano tuner from Portland, had reached the final point of the tour where the guide invited guests to rub a "wishing stone" before exiting. Gruber, uninterested, kept on moving, but his wife Norma stopped long enough to touch the polished rock. Eyeing her, he turned back and asked what she was doing. "Just wishing that something would come of your idea," she replied.

Gruber's idea involved the mass production of color 3-D images (up until this point, stills of this ilk only existed in black-and-white) and an affordable compact viewer through which they could be seen. A stereo enthusiast, Gruber had rigged up a makeshift tripod-mounted dual lens camera (actually, it was two cameras he had tied together) and had it on his shoulder when he walked out of the cave and directly in front of Harold Graves.

Talk about being in the right place at the right time.

Graves was president of Sawyer's, a local photofinishing and postcard company always on the lookout for a new idea. Intrigued by Gruber's homemade equipment, he struck up a conversation, and reportedly, by the next morning, the two men had struck a deal. While Gruber's hope was that he would make enough money to afford a two-week vacation every year, Graves explained that he had to sink all the resources he had into buying machinery and supplies; so instead of paying him a fee, he could only offer Gruber a percentage of any future profits.

Lucky Break #2.

By late 1939, the first viewers (which looked much like a pair of opera glasses) and the first set of reels (fifteen in all and all of them scenic) had been produced and began to appear in camera shops around Portland. Wanting time to build up inventory, Sawyer did not introduce the View-Master (a name, by the way, which Gruber hated, because he felt it sounded, *a la* Mixmaster and Toastmaster, too much like a kitchen appliance) nationally until the New York and San Francisco World's Fairs the following year. It was an immediate hit and the thousand dealers across the country sold out as fast as the stock came in.

World War II, however, almost put an end to all this. Shortages of film, plastic, and paper threatened to make the product obsolete—and would have had the Army and Navy not picked up on its potential as a training tool. Between 1942 and 1945, about 100,000 viewers and five to six million reels were ordered by the military, covering such topics as ship identification and aircraft gunnery. Better yet, the job assured the plant a supply of raw materials and a ready-and-waiting workforce once full production resumed post-war.

The five years that followed were no doubt the most significant: The viewer was redesigned, so that reels could be easily inserted through a slit in the top, not by (as in earlier models) having to open the front like a camera. The company moved into larger facilities in nearby Beaverton (not only allowing them to more than quadruple the number of their dealers, but creating perhaps the first suburban industrial park). And acting on their success with a series of reels depicting fairy tales using three-dimensional hand-sculpted figures and detailed background dioramas, Sawyer's purchased Tru-Vue, a rival filmstrip manufacturer who just happened to own the stereo license to the Disney characters. This did more than eliminate their only serious competition. It marked the beginning of the evolution of the View-Master into a full-time children's toy.

Although for the last thirty-five years the majority of their business has been in toy stores (save the scenic and "attractions" reels, which no souvenir shop worth its salt would be without), View-Master does—as they always did—a considerable business in special orders. These custom-made commercial reels are usually for advertising or promotional purposes (Nicole Miller has used them to show store buyers her newest clothing line; Marriott sent them out to corporate clients to tout their convention and banquet facilities). But they've also found their way into restaurants (as 3-D menus in the 1950s at the Ganzt Steak House in Sioux City and today at the Rainforest Cafe in the Mall of America), medical schools (as a teaching tool for brain and eye surgery techniques) and real estate offices (Warning: bathrooms may be smaller than they appear).

Highly sought after by collectors, these reels hold an important place in View-Master history in that the first reel ever produced was a commercial one—for a construction company who wanted to publicize their roofing and siding business.

While every View-Master reel has fourteen frames, in actuality each reel provides only seven separate images, since seeing in 3-D requires one visual for each eye. Packets normally contain three reels, so a story has to be told in twenty-one scenes.

When View-Master went public in the mid-1980s, the stock certificates were printed in 3-D.

The reel today remains exactly as it was when Sawyer first produced it in 1939, so old reels work in new viewers and old viewers can accommodate new reels. A source for both (which means you can once again visit Disneyland as it was in 1960) is *Inside 3-D*, a combination magazine, mail order, and auction catalog that sells everything View-Master, plus stereo cameras, projectors, and lenticulars.

Contact 3-D From Dalia, P.O. Box 492, Corte Madera, CA 94925; (415) 924-3356.

whee-lo

Invented in Patterson, New Jersey, in 1953, the Whee-lo consisted of a curved piece of wire and a $2^{1}/_{2}$-inch red plastic wheel that spun up, down, and all around its edge without ever falling off. Some kids credited this to the type of metal or the holes in the wheel. Many reasoned it had to do with centrifugal force. Others swore it was all in the wrist.

None of them were right (Okay, if you must know: a small magnet runs through the core of the wheel, which allows it to roll continuously along the wire—and stay there). But the magic of the Whee-lo had nothing to do with how it worked. The real magic was that it only *looked* difficult, which meant it gave all of us—no matter how short or tall, fat, or thin—the chance to show our stuff.

it curves!

wiffle **BALL**

Growing up in fifties suburbia (in his case, Fairfield, Conneticut), David Mullany, Jr., was cursed with a boy's worst nightmare: a backyard too small to play baseball. But rather than let that stop him, he simply improvised a game of his own, using a sawed-off broom handle and a plastic golf ball. The advantage was that even when he really connected, the plastic ball didn't have the weight to go very far. The frustration was no matter how hard that he threw, a ball this light wouldn't curve. Not that that stopped him from trying. However, these repeated attempts to put some motion in his pitch started to worry his dad, a former semipro player who understood his kid's passion, but who had questions about what the constant wrist-snapping might be doing to his arm. The answer was to build a better ball.

Thanks to a contact at a nearby cosmetics factory, Mullany, Sr., was given some plastic moldings (made to package Coty perfume bottles) that were round, hollow, and just slightly smaller than base-balls. Sitting down at the kitchen table, he took a razor blade and began cutting various-sized holes in each, hoping to come up with a pattern that would let the right amount of air through to make it curve. The next morning, David, Jr., put them to the test, announcing that the one which had the eight oblong holes centered at one end worked particularly well.

So well that Mullany, whose firm manufacturing car polish was in trouble, decided to market it. He borrowed money, mortgaged the house, and filed for U.S. patent #2,776,139—the Wiffle ball. The name was derived from the word *whiff*, popular slang in 1953 for striking out. His new product would do anything but.

How They Do It:

Every other baseball may currently be manufactured in the Far East, but the Wiffle remains all-American. In a small Conneticut factory, beads of plastic are mixed with white powder (for coloring), then melted into a liquid and molded into one of two halves. Next, a solid half is welded with a perforated half, leaving a small ring around the middle that has to be trimmed by hand. From start to finish, the entire process takes about five seconds.

Although the ball was never intended to cross the baseline into the major leagues, Kevin Mitchell, a major league baseball player, credits his ability to hit a curve to years of playing Wiffle. In their book *The Final Days*, Woodward and Bernstein reported that while the Nixon administration was crumbling, David Eisenhower would try and ease tensions by gathering all the president's men for rounds of "Home Run Derby." The goal was to hit a Wiffle over the fence of the White House tennis courts. And in Cincinnati, there are four ball fields devoted solely to Wiffle, although none are as elaborate as the park in Frederick, Maryland (no longer operational), which came complete with bleachers, automatic scoreboard, state-of-the-art lighting and concession stands.

As a company, The Wiffle Ball, Inc., is unique in the toy industry because they do not advertise. There was, however, one exception: a 1960 TV commercial with New York Yankees pitcher Whitey Ford. Interestingly, sales increased—but not substantially enough to compensate for the cost of the ads.

WOOLY *willy*

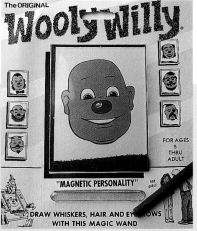

Poking around the offices at Smethport Specialty, a company that made classic horseshoe-shaped magnets as well as spinning tops and other metal playthings, Don Herzog, the ten-year-old son of the company founder, was impressed by a prototype for a toy that would allow you to create funny expressions over a line drawing of an old maid school teacher's face by moving iron dust with a magnetic stylus. But because the designers couldn't keep the plastic covering holding the dust secured, the project had been scrapped. Eighteen years later, at a packaging show in 1951, Herzog saw a vaccumn-forming piece of equipment that could mold plastic containers that wouldn't leak. Reminded of the toy idea he had loved as a kid, he created a sample and called it Wooly Willy.

While the magnetic dust didn't fall out, there were other problems. The head buyer at Woolworth's told him no one would spend money on a "bunch of cold powder underneath a piece of cellophane"; the plastic covering would cloud over after continued use; and static electricity made it hard to draw. But Herzog persisted, ironed out the kinks, and finally got the G. C. Murphy five-and-dime chain to put six dozen in each of their sixteen stores. A year later, Wooly Willy was everywhere...including Woolworth's. Smethport followed Wooly's success with variations on the original—the larger-sized Dapper Dan, and Brunette Betty, a female version that, unlike the other two, is no longer being manufactured.

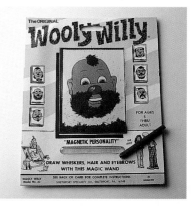

Wooly Willy was originally drawn by a postal worker in Bradford, Pennsylvania, who modeled the face after his neighbor two doors down. It's a face that remains unchanged today and one so familiar it was given a starrring role in an ad campaign for The Hair Club For Men.

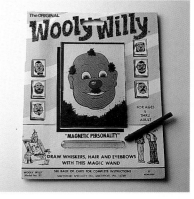

ACKNOWLEDGMENTS

For all its fun and games, the toy industry is serious business—highly proprietary, extremely competitive, and tight-lipped when it comes to facts, figures, and information. Not exactly welcome news when you're trying to write a book. So, my gratitude to all those whose files, faxes, photos, and phone calls helped see this project through—in particular *Chris Adams* (Novelty Gags), *Bill Bean* (Erector Set), *Evelyn Burkhalter* (Barbie), *Michael Caffrey* (Duncan Yo-Yo), *Karen Carzo* (Nerf), *Tom Cureton and Betty James* (Slinky), *Jane Davies* (View-Master), *Brad Drexler and Susan Tucker* (Crayola Crayons, Silly Putty), *Kim Gruelle* (Raggedy Ann), *Katherine Ingham* (Colorforms), *Rich Ingoldsby* (Magic Rocks), *Frank Kappler* (Frisbee), *Steve Levine* (Ant Farm), *Eva Lykkegaard* (Lego), *Mark Morris* (The Game of Life & Other Games), *David and Stephen Mullany* (Wiffle Ball), *Sandra Bogunia Spinatsch* (Etch A Sketch), *Craig Strange* (Tinkertoy), *Ann Sharma* (Flexible Flyer, Roadmaster), *and Judy Wenzel* (Labyrinth).

PLUS SPECIAL THANKS TO:

Jodi Levin at Toy Manufacturers of America, who ended every conversation with, "I'm sorry I couldn't help more," yet each time never failed to point me in the right direction.

Patti Breitman, Leah Komaiko, Brenda Wilson, and Leslie Zerg for their advice, well thought out criticisms, comments, and suggestions.

Jay Schaefer, Caroline Herter, Michael Carabetta, and Chronicle Books for inviting me over to play with them.

And Eckeley and Horace, without whose guidance I never would have eaten Play-Doh, colored on the dining room walls, or written four-letter words on an Etch A Sketch.

CREDITS